The Chalet School 12

FREE GIFTS FROM
THE ARMADA COLLECTORS' CLUB

Look out for these tokens in your favourite Armada series! All you need to do to receive a special FREE GIFT is collect 6 tokens in the same series and send them off to the address below with a postcard marked with your name and address including postcode. Start collecting today!

The Chalet School series by Elinor M. Brent-Dyer

The Chalet School at War

Elinor M. Brent-Dyer

Armada
An Imprint of HarperCollins*Publishers*

First published in 1941 by W & R Chambers Ltd
as *The Chalet School Goes to It*
First published in paperback in 1988 by
William Collins Sons & Co. Ltd
This impression 1992

Armada is an imprint of HarperCollins Children's Books,
a division of HarperCollins Publishers Ltd,
77–85 Fulham Palace Road, Hammersmith,
London W6 8JB

Printed and bound in Great Britain by
HarperCollins Book Manufacturing Ltd, Glasgow.

To Avary Nancy Ovens, dearest of friends

Contents

CHAPTER 1

Fresh Plans

"I don't like it at all," said Miss Annersley, "not in the least."

Miss Wilson, geography and science mistress of the Chalet School, put her elbows on the table and cupped her face in her hands. "Don't you think you are worrying rather needlessly, Hilda? After all, it was only one plane— and crippled at that."

"If one can get here—no matter how—others can. We are very near the Continent, and with other people's children—" Miss Annersley stopped speaking, and the staff looked at each other.

"But if the parents are willing to risk it, I don't see why *you* should bother," argued pretty Miss Stewart who was history mistress.

"How can I help it? No, it's no use. I do feel that we ought to move somewhere further away. I may be all wrong. There may never be any here at all—or no more than we've already had. At the same time, we may be bombed out of existence, and I can't risk it. Madge!" She turned to the slight, graceful woman who sat at the other end of the long table, knitting a long grey scarf. "What do *you* think about it all? Am I not right in what I say?"

The rest of the staff followed her example and gazed eagerly at Mrs Russell, for she was the owner of the school and, as such, had the casting vote in all matters of importance.

Madge Russell laid down her work. "Jem and I discussed it last week," she said gravely. "We knew that it must come up. He insists that I shall take all our nurseryful to England as soon as possible. In that case, I can scarcely leave the school here. As Hilda says, it's a case of other people's children. If ours go, then they must go too. Jack Maynard

9

agrees. He is sending Joey and the triplets away as soon after Easter as possible—even, it may be, before.''

''Joey won't like that,'' said Miss Wilson shrewdly. ''She loves her pretty home. And where will they go, Madge? Pretty Maids is out of the question now, I imagine.''

''Oh, quite impossible. If the old folk had been living, it would have been the obvious solution, for you know how they adored her, and she loved them dearly. But now that they are gone, and Mrs Robert and the Major are in possession, it's out of the question, as you say. None of the Maynards have ever liked poor Lydia, and she is a most uncomfortable person, I admit. She has always resented the fact that, since Rolf's death, Jack is his brother's heir; and since the coming of the triplets, it's been worse. Bob Maynard wrote a charming letter to Jo, but Lydia has taken no notice whatsoever.''

''Spite and jealousy!'' interjected a small, spare woman in nurse's uniform, who sat near by.

Madge Russell shook her head. ''I think a good deal of it comes from poor little Rolf's tragedy. You see, their doctor told Lydia that she had only herself to blame. If the boy had ever been taught obedience, the accident need not have happened. But Lydia gave in to him in every way, and Bob himself was too much away with his regiment to interfere. As it is, Rolf disobeyed a direct command, and was killed.''

''Well, as things are today, Mrs Robert might have had to worry about him in one of the services,'' observed Miss Wilson. ''He'd have been nearly nineteen now, wouldn't he? But Madge, it's six years ago since it happened. Jack and Joey were both in the Tyrol at the time—Joey was at school! How *can* Mrs Robert vent it on them?''

''Because that's Lydia Maynard all over,'' put in Miss Stewart. ''She was at school with my sister Nancy, and Nancy told me that if anything went wrong, Lydia always took it out on someone else.''

''Don't let's discuss it,'' said Mrs Russell. ''The thing we've got to decide is what we are going to do with the school. That's enough.''

"Quite," agreed Miss Wilson, pushing a strand of her curly white hair out of her eyes. "Are we likely to take any of the day children with us, does anyone know?"

"It all depends on where we go. The Lucys are leaving. They are closing Les Arbres for the duration, taking what furniture they need with them and storing the rest. They've got a house outside Armiford to be near the Ozannes—you remember Paul Ozanne got the Recordership there. If we can get anywhere near them, we shall keep the three Lucy children and the Ozanne twins. And the Willoughbys are going to Surrey. Both his and her people live there; and Rosamund Willoughby told me yesterday that if we could get a place either near them or near Armiford, Toby and Blossom should come to us as before."

"It'll be difficult getting anywhere, won't it?" queried Miss Stewart thoughtfully. "We need rather a big place, you see."

"Not nearly so difficult as it will be later on," replied the Head. "If we can get away at once, I should think we might get—Hello! *Joey*! Where did you come from? We didn't expect you."

"Jack ran me over here in the car," said the tall, dark girl, who had just entered the room, her arms full of red-headed babies. "I knew you were having a meeting to discuss the latest problem, and I wasn't going to be out of it—no fear! Here you are, Nell! Here's your goddaughter. Con, here's yours. Yes, Simone, you may have Margot for the present." And she dealt out a baby to each of the persons named before she sank into the chair the last person had drawn up to the table for her. "Well? Come to any decision yet?"

"Just that it will be wiser to move the school at once."

Jo Maynard nodded thoughtfully. "I agree. I'm going myself in three weeks' time. Jack insists on it. We had it out last night, and we agreed that it wouldn't be right to risk the children. I really came today to tell you about it."

"I didn't know Jack meant to speak to you yet," said her sister. "He and Jem talked it over last week, and Jem told me."

"So he said. I hate the idea of leaving Guernsey when we've settled down so happily. Still, as Jack says, it'll be a good deal easier for him to get to us, and he won't have to worry quite so much about what's happening to us while he's away. Anyhow," added Jo gravely, "Jack and the children are really what makes home for me now. So long as I have them, it doesn't matter too much where we are."

Simone Lecoutier, on whose left hand gleamed a very new diamond ring, smiled sympathetically at her friend over little Margot's head, and Miss Stewart, whose own marriage had had to be postponed because of the war, looked down, a sudden shadow on her face. Miss Annersley saw, and changed the topic as quickly as she could.

"Well, we are all agreed, I suppose? The next thing to decide is—oh bother! There's the bell! I hope it's no one to see me."

Three minutes later, Michelle, the pretty Guernsey maid, came to announce that a gentleman, who said his business was urgent, was asking for Miss Annersley. She handed over his card, and the Head glanced at it. " 'The Rev Ernest Howell.' Who on earth can he be? Near Armiford! What a strange coincidence!"

"Your hair's coming down at that side," said Jo. "Pin it up, do, or he'll think you most untidy. That's better! Now trot off, and get rid of him as soon as you can, and come back."

Miss Annersley laughed, and left the room, and the rest settled down to the discussion of minor school matters while she was gone. It was a good half-hour before she returned, bringing with her a slight, black-eyed man in the dress of a naval chaplain. He was in his thirties, and there was an anxious look on his face. The Head introduced him to Mrs Russell, and then to the staff *en masse*. He was given a chair, while the startled mistresses eyed him, wondering what had brought him to the staff meeting. They had not long to wonder. The Head took her seat, and then spoke, her cheeks flushed, her eyes shining. "Listen, everyone! Mr Howell has come to ask us to take charge of his little sister, and to offer us the loan of his house, Plas Howell in Armishire, for the duration of the war.''

For a moment they were all stunned to silence. Then Jo, the ever-ready, chipped in. ''Not really? Whatever makes you do that, Mr Howell? It'll be a boon and a blessing, I can assure you. But what *has* put it into your head?''

''Your brother-in-law,'' he told her, ''if, as I think you must be, you are Mrs Jack Maynard. I've seen photos of you at Pretty Maids.''

''*Bob* did?' Jo was almost robbed of breath. ''You know him, then?''

''At school with him,'' returned the stranger. He cast an interested glance on the three babies, who were fast asleep. ''Are these the famous triplets? What jolly little kids!''

''Not bad, are they? That's Mary Constance; that one is Mary Helena; and this one is my baby of all, Mary Margaret.'' Jo introduced her daughters in would-be casual tones.

Feeling that it was time the meeting came down to brass tacks, Mrs Russell took a hand. ''We are very pleased to see you, Mr Howell. But what is the real meaning of Miss Annersley's remark? You can't mean that you are offering us a house for the school?''

''Just that,'' he said. ''You see, it's this way. When all of us but my young sister Nesta were grown-up, our father married again—our own mother died when Nesta was born—a very pretty girl. They had one little girl, Guenever, or Gwensi, as we call her. Before that, our stepmother brought Nesta through a bad attack of pneumonia, and saved her life. Nesta is a good deal younger than the rest of us, and we'd always made a pet of her, so you can guess our feelings towards Gwen—our stepmother. When she and my father were drowned, yachting, when Gwensi was only four, we all made up our minds that we'd do by her baby as she'd done by ours. At that time, I was in a curacy in Armiford, and shortly after, I was offered the living of Howell Village. My godfather—a splendid old chap—lived near by, and he insisted that I should accept. I went, and took Gwensi with me, as I was the only one who could offer her a home. The eldest of us, my brother David, is in the Navy, and though he is married, his wife is delicate, and knows nothing about children. Olwen, who comes next to him, was living at Goathland, which the doctors thought too bracing for Gwensi, who isn't strong. Evan, who comes next to me, was house-surgeon at one of the London hospitals, and Nesta is a nurse. So, you see, it left me. When my godfather died, three years ago, he left me everything—he was an old bachelor—including Plas Howell, which is a huge old place, built in the days when seventeen or eighteen was quite a usual size for a family. I moved up there, partly to give Gwensi the benefit of the fresher air—Howell Village lies in the hollow—and partly because it was easier than putting in a caretaker. Now I am accepted as a naval chaplain, my locum will use the rectory, which is more than big enough for him and his wife and their two girls. I was staying at Pretty Maids with Bob Maynard, who is an old pal of mine, and said I didn't know what to do with Gwensi. He suggested sending her here; but I don't like the notion of her being so near the Continent. Then he proposed that I should offer the school Plas Howell for the duration, and keep her where she was. It seems the best idea of all. What do you think of it?"

"I like Bob's nerve," commented his sister-in-law. "I notice he's said nothing about Pretty Maids."

"Plas Howell on the borders of Wales would be a jolly sight safer than even the New Forest," retorted the visitor. "Oh, I don't say that there's much risk of their getting there. But—you never know. France might just conceivably crack up—they've had a long wait, and that's bad for the nerves. And there's a lot of jiggery-pokery going on in political circles, I believe. Anyhow—there's the offer—Plas Howell with young Gwensi attached to it. What do you say?"

"It's rather a big question to settle in a hurry, isn't it?" said Miss Wilson. "I mean, to remove an entire school is a big job."

"It's one that will have to be done, though," said Madge. "We've all agreed on that. As for this offer of Mr Howell's, I consider it providential. You can't do better than accept, Hilda. The Ozannes and the Lucys are going to be in Armiford, so we should keep the children."

"Plas Howell is fourteen miles or so from Armiford," said Mr Howell. "Ozanne? Isn't that the new Recorder?"

'Yes, Paul Ozanne is the new Recorder for Armiford. Mrs Lucy is his wife's sister, and as Mr Lucy is in the R.A.F., he insists on their removing to England. The Ozanne twin girls and the two eldest Lucy children are pupils here."

"And so are the little Chesters," put in Joey. "Anne Chester is another Temple girl. D'you think Peter will send Anne and the kids to England, too, Madge? We'd keep Beth and Nancy and the twins then."

Mr Howell's eyes wandered to her tiny daughters, and he grinned. "*More* twins? You do seem to go in for quantity over here."

Jo gave him grin for grin. "We do. My sister has three singles. But we have a brother—*her* twin, by the way—and Peggy and Rix are here, as well as Bride and Jacky, who are singles too. I'm the only one to rise to triplets. They caused quite a sensation when they arrived."

"I'm sure they did," agreed the visitor. "Well, Miss Annersley, what do you say? This is March, so I assume you will be breaking up before long. Will you accept my offer and move during the holidays? I shall be thankful if you will agree, for Gwensi is a good deal of a problem as you may guess. We are singularly devoid of relatives except for our immediate family. Olwen—my eldest sister—has closed her house and is living in rooms in Rugby to be near her boys who are at the school, so she is no use. And David's wife is the last person to have charge of a child who, I must admit, isn't easy to deal with."

Miss Annersley glanced across at Mrs Russell. "We had better have a quiet discussion about ways and means before we decide anything," she said slowly. "On the face of it, the offer is a marvellous one. But we must go into more detail before we close with it. Will you come with Mrs Russell and me to my study, Mr Howell, and then we can see what arrangements can be made. I may say," she added, taking pity on his fallen face, "that I feel strongly inclined to say 'yes'. But we must be businesslike—so will you come?"

He rose to his feet. "I see your point. But I do hope you will agree."

"So do I," said Joey unexpectedly. "Hurry up and decide, you people, because Jack will be coming for me in a few minutes, and I want to know before we go."

And, to cut matters short, in half an hour's time, the trio returned to the staff room to say that it was all settled, and the Chalet School would remove once more, this time to Plas Howell, where, it was hoped, they would find a certain amount of peace and security for the rest of the war.

CHAPTER 2

Joey Departs

It was the Wednesday of Easter week. Joey Maynard was standing pensively in the hall of Les Rosiers, the home in Guernsey that she had so loved, her arms full of rugs, while in the big pram nearby lay the precious triplets. They were bonny babies, six months old, with dark-red hair, the lovely colouring that goes with such hair, and round, dimpled faces. The eldest, little Helena, looked out at the world from eyes of soft grey, while Constance, who came next, had eyes of deepest brown, and Margot, the youngest, smiled on all with eyes of true forget-me-not blue. "And a mercy it is!" as their mother once remarked. "If they'd been all alike, I'd never have known one from the other. As it is, I've no difficulty so long as they're awake;" a remark which called down on her devoted head the outcries of her sister and her friends, Mrs Ozanne, Mrs Chester, and Mrs Lucy.

Mrs Maynard was leaving Guernsey early, for a house had fallen vacant in Howell Village, and as she had to take it at once, she decided that she might as well remove and get it over. Mrs Russell had taken her own trio and her brother Dick Bettany's quartet across the week before, to take up residence in an old Georgian hunting lodge at the top of a hill not far from the village. The Ozannes had also gone, and with them went little Mrs Lucy and her adopted sister, Nan Blakeney, and the five Lucy youngsters. Les Arbres, the pretty old house where the four younger Lucy children had been born, had been denuded of almost everything, since most of the furniture had gone to England, where a house not far from Plas Howell had been rented, and the old home was in the hands of caretakers now.

"What an exodus it is!" sighed Joey aloud. "The school will be coming next, I suppose—unless Dr Peter sends Anne

17

and the children to the Ozannes before then.''

A light step behind her made her turn. She saw her little adopted sister, Robin Humphries, standing there. Robin was nearly sixteen, a slight, delicate-looking girl, with deep brown eyes, and thick black curls tied back from a face of almost angelic loveliness with a big bow. Joey's heart contracted as she met the smile on the sensitive lips, and she dropped the rugs, and caught the girl to her.

''Robin, my darling, I wish you were coming with me now.''

''So do I,'' said Robin, nestling up to her. ''But after all, Joey, I'm a prefect now. I couldn't desert the school, could I? And we shall come after you before long. Don't look so worried, dearest. Miss Annersley and the rest of the staff will look after us quite well.''

''I don't know.'' Joey was in an emotional state, and she had always loved the Robin with her whole heart. ''I hate leaving you like this. We've never been separated before. What shall I do without you and Daisy to help me with the babes?'' And she glanced across at her daughters who were sleeping in the pram. ''Oh, Rob, I shall leave half my heart here until you come to me in England!''

Robin laughed. ''I wish Jack could hear you! As for what you will do, you will have Frieda to help you. And after all, Jo, the Germans may never reach here. We may be getting up scares for no reason at all.''

''I only hope it *is* so!'' said Jo fervently.

''We must hope it is. Now here comes Jem with the car. How are you going to get the pram into it?''

''Rob! Talk sense! It's staying behind. They're only there because there wasn't anywhere else for them to sleep. I can't carry them *all* the time—they're *some* weight now!'' And Joey stepped across the fallen rugs to bend over the pram and lift out her youngest daughter. Robin took the baby in her arms, and bent over her, eyes glowing with love as she held the small thing close, and touched her lips very tenderly and softly to the silky waves of red hair.

''You ought to have had dark-haired babies, Jo. The next

18

must be like you, darling. It looks so funny for you to have red-haired children!"

"Mercy! Don't talk of another till I've got these three safely past teething and weaning, and all the rest of the baby bothers!" protested Jo. "They're only just six months old now. Give me a year or two, my child!"

"Peggy and Rix are barely eleven months older than Bride," Robin pointed out. "But I won't tease you just now. Here's Jem, wondering what on earth he can do about the pram."

Dr Russell, Jo's brother-in-law and the Robin's guardian since she was an orphan, regarded the big pram with dismayed eyes as he stood at the open door. "Goodness, Jo! D'you expect me to take that pantechnicon of yours on the car?"

"Never thought about it," returned Jo equably as she lifted her two remaining daughters from it with a dexterity born of much practice. "It will stay here and come over with Anna on the boat. Is Nigel there, Jem?"

"Waiting for you, so you'd better hurry. Here, give me Len!"

"No, thanks, I've got them quite comfortably. You bring those rugs and pillows. Come on, Rob. The sooner it's over, the sooner we shall be at the other side." Jo walked to the door, followed by Robin. She stood aside to let the younger girl pass out first, and then cast a wistful glance round the dismantled hall. "Oh, Jem, it is so miserable! I've been so happy here, and I *did* think I was settled for a few years after all our alarums and excursions in the Tyrol and our escape from it. I could *skin* Hitler for all this!" she added viciously.

"So could a good many other folk," agreed the doctor as he collected the pillows and rugs from the floor. "Is that the lot? You're sure of it? Then come along, and don't keep me waiting while you moan over a house you may come back to any day. Nigel is fussing to get off, and I don't blame him. Remember, you've got to get across the Channel, and it's none too healthy just now."

19

Jo shrugged her shoulders as well as she could for the babies in her arms, and followed him down the long garden path to the big car at the gate. Robin was already there, little Margot safely settled into a corner. She held out her arms, and Jo gave her Len to tuck in, and followed with Connie, while the doctor packed away the rugs and pillows.

"Are you and Daisy ready, Rob?" he asked.

Robin nodded. "Daisy's just getting our bicycles out, and we're going straight back to school when Anna's locked up," she explained. "The Head only gave us leave to see Joey off. We've got to get back as soon as possible after she's gone. And here's Daisy," she added, as a yellow-headed, long-legged irresponsible of thirteen came round the corner of the house, carefully wheeling two bicycles. "What ages you've been, Daisy. What have you been doing?"

"Pumping up both our back tyres," said Daisy virtuously. "Oh is Jo off now? Jo, I do hate to see you and the triplets going!"

"No more than I hate *going*," sighed Jo as she stooped to receive Daisy's kisses. "Never mind, Daisy girl! Soon the school will be coming over, and then you and Rob are to live with me. The house is quite a good size, Auntie Madge tells me, so there'll be room for you both. It'll be rather a long journey for you to school every day, even with your cycles; but I suppose you won't mind that?"

"Not in the least. And it would be horrid to be boarders when the triplets are growing so quickly. Must you go, Uncle Jem? Then goodbye, Joey. Take care of the babies. Oh, how I *hate* having to leave Guernsey." And the tears came to Daisy's blue eyes as she spoke.

Jo bent to kiss her again. "It's only for a short time, we hope, darling. And you and the rest will be following us to England very soon. Just think, Daisy! You're an English girl, and you've never seen your own country yet, what with spending all your early years in Australia, and then in the Tyrol, and now Guernsey. It's high time you knew something about your own country. Now I *must* say goodbye, darling. Look after Primula for us, and be very good. Remember, you and Robin are among the few *really* Chalet School girls left. You've got to set the standard—keep the flag flying, in fact,'' she added with a little choke as she thought of all that had chanced to the school her sister had built up in the Tyrol, the school which they both loved so dearly.

Daisy nodded, and forced back the tears. There was a final hug to each of the schoolgirls, and then Jo, not trusting herself for any more, got into the car beside her babies; the doors were shut; and Jem, who had been waiting patiently at the wheel, drove off, taking her from the home she had loved so much.

"Why is Nigel in such a hurry to get off, Jem?" asked Jo when she had finally succeeded in swallowing the inconvenient lump in her throat and generally composing herself.

The doctor was busy negotiating a passage between a lorry and a motorcycle, so he did not answer for a moment or two. Then, "Submarines!" he flung curtly at her over his shoulder.

"*Jem*! What about my babies?"

"Don't worry. Nigel has good look-outs. And you and your babies *must* leave this place, and you'll be as safe at sea as in the air—and there isn't any other way that I know of of getting back to England."

"I shan't know a moment's peace till we *are* there."

"I didn't—last week," he retorted grimly.

Joey was silenced. The previous week, when her sister and all the nieces and nephews save Daisy and Primula Venables, the children of the doctor's dead sister, had gone, had been a trying one for them all. She had worried till the wire came saying that the party had arrived safely. Now she could realize what her sister must have gone through with the seven children until they were safely ashore. And her great friend Janie Lucy had gone through it too for she had five small people, and had taken her sister Anne's elder family as well, leaving Mrs Chester with only Beth, the first-born of the crowd, and Barbara, the baby.

"Thank Heaven I've only the triplets to worry about!" she thought, as she sat looking her farewells at the countryside. "Oh dear! When shall I see it all again? I could cry to think of it all!"

But at this point, her brother-in-law was speaking to her, and she had to listen to him. "I'm thankful to get you off, Joey. The Gestapo have long memories, and you know what happened when they marched into Austria."

"Yes, but they'll never associate Mrs Jack Maynard with Joey Bettany. And what about Bill? If I'm in danger, isn't she just as much?"

"Just as much," agreed the doctor. "Bill crosses with you. You will find her waiting for you on the *Sea Witch*—at least, I hope so. She was told to be there by eleven sharp."

Then he said no more, for they had entered a narrow lane, leading down to the shore, and he needed all his skill to manoeuvre the car safely down the road. They reached their destination at length, and Joey gave an exclamation as she saw, well out to sea, and away from the treacherous coast, the outlines of the big steam—yacht that was to bear her and her babies and Miss Wilson to the comparative safety of England.

A dinghy was drawn up on the beach, and beside it stood a tall, fair-haired man—Nigel Willoughby, whose wife was another of her closest friends in Guernsey. From the yacht, she could see someone waving a streamer. Then the car stopped, and she had to hurry out, while Jem passed out the babies one by one.

"You go on," he told her. "I'll bring the rest of the traps."

Joey made her way slowly over the soft sand to Nigel Willoughby, who was directing his men to push the boat into the water. He looked up as she approached, and gave her a nod. "Glad to see you. Come along! Give me the babies to hold while you get in, and I'll pass them to you."

"*Can* you—hold them, I mean?" queried Jo doubtfully.

Nigel's set face relaxed into a grin as he replied, "That's an insult. Haven't I three of my own?"

"Yes, but separately," retorted Jo. "Well, don't drop them. That's all I ask." And she relinquished her burden into his long arms, and sprang from the shore to the gunwale of the boat, where one of the men caught and steadied her till she was able to sit down in the stern. Then Nigel came wading ankle-deep through the water, and deposited the babies in her lap. He returned for the wraps and the rest of Jo's light luggage. There was a call of "Goodbye!" and the owner of the *Sea Witch* was taking the rudder-lines in his hands, while his men pulled steadily away from the shore towards the yacht.

Tears stood in Joey's dark eyes as she looked back, but she kept them from falling; and in a very few minutes they were pulling alongside the yacht, where Miss Wilson and her dearest friend, Frieda von Ahlen, were hanging over the rail, waving excitedly to her.

"At last!" exclaimed the former, as Joey, bearing one baby, mounted the companionway. "What ages you've been, Joey!'

"So would you if you had three babies to look after!" retorted Jo, who had managed to recover herself by this time. "Frieda, I'm thankful to see you. With the three of us, we ought to be able to manage the infants all right, whatever turns up. Nell, you may have charge of your goddaughter, and Frieda must look after Connie. I'll see to Margot. Oh, *thank* you, Nigel!" as that gentleman came on deck, bearing little Connie. "Take her, Frieda liebchen."

Frieda, a slender, fair girl, with the apple-blossom colouring of her north Tyrolean ancestry, and eyes as blue as little Margot's, took the brown-eyed baby from Mr Willoughby, and then, at the suggestion of Miss Wilson, who was already cuddling little Len, they made a move for the cabin where Joey might sit down and collect herself.

Twenty minutes later they were bowling over the waves, for a fresh breeze was blowing, and the *Sea Witch* heeled over gaily as it caught her sails. In the cabin, Joey was being inducted into her life-belt, and being informed by Nigel Willoughby that she must retain it until they reached shore again.

23

"And how long will that be?" she enquired.

"It all depends. There's no knowing what twists and turns we may have to take if the Nazis have any of their blinking U-boats about."

"Can't you give me *some* idea? I mean—what about the babies?"

Nigel frowned. "I'd forgotten. That's a complication. We may be anything up to two days or so. Can't you manage anyhow, Joey?"

"Talk sense! Apart from anything else, how would *you* like to be cuddled up against a thing like this? And they're *all* teething. Of course, they may not be bothered. But if they are, I can tell you they have all got the healthiest lungs."

"I give up," he said helplessly. "You must contrive somehow." And he left the cabin to go on deck.

"Isn't that just like a man?" demanded Joey of her two friends. "Well, they seem disposed to sleep at the moment. Let's hope it lasts for a while. Anyhow, I fed them just before we left the house, so they oughtn't to want anything for a few hours yet. Let's put them into the basket for the present, and then we can talk. They'll be much more comfy that way."

She produced the big basket in which the triplets were accustomed to being carried about, since, as she had once said, three made more of an armful than was convenient any other way, and the babies were laid in it, still fast asleep. Then the three friends gathered round, prepared each to snatch up one baby at a moment's notice, and they discussed the latest developments of the situation.

"I wish to heaven the school were well away," said Miss Wilson suddenly.

"Bill! This from you? I thought you were under the impression that everyone was being needlessly careful."

"I was. But, somehow—oh, I don't know. I suppose it's having to be on the run again. Anyhow, I shall be thankful when we're all at Plas Gwyn. We ought to be safe enough there, anyhow. From all accounts it's deep in the heart of the country, and near no military target."

"Supposing they use parachute troops as they've been doing in Norway?" suggested Frieda.

"They won't find it nearly so easy with us. For one thing, we've got the sea between us and them. For another, it's right at the wrong side of England for them. And the R.A.F. are absolutely on the spot—I say! We seem to be dithering about a good deal, don't we? I wonder if anything's up?" As she spoke, Joey's hand crept to the big basket where the three babies still slept peacefully, and Miss Wilson's followed hers, while Frieda jumped up as well as she could for her cumbersome lifebelt, and ran to the door to make enquiries.

"There is nothing wrong," she reported when she came back. "Mr Willoughby says that he is only tacking on general principles. Joey, what does he mean—'tacking'?"

"Going from side to side—a sort of zigzag," said Joey. "It would make it more difficult to hit us than if we were set on a straight course."

They fell silent for a little after that. Then Margot waked and whimpered to be taken up, and her cries disturbed the other two, so they were busy with the children for a little. But when at length the three were put back into their basket, fed and soothed and asleep again, "Bill" reverted to the former topic of conversation.

"It's bad enough bringing three tiny babies across the Channel at such a time. But think what it will be with all those girls. You know I do feel that I ought to go back after I've seen you people all safely to Howell Village, and give a helping hand."

Before anyone could reply, the vessel changed course so violently and suddenly that it was only by an effort that they saved themselves from being flung on to the floor.

"It's a U-boat!" cried Joey, grabbing the basket. "Here's Connie, Frieda! Nell, take Len. Ought we to stay here—"

Nigel himself appeared in the doorway to answer her question. "On deck at once, all three of you! Quick!"

He hustled them out of the cabin, each clutching her baby

25

to her. The three tinies, rudely awakened, set up loud yells, but no one paid any attention to them. Nigel pushed the three women towards the boat slung from the davits on the port side of the vessel, and then shoved them on to the deck. "Keep down," he told them curtly. "At the word, leap into the boat. Don't wait for anything. There's a German about!"

Then he left them, and rushed off to where his men were uncovering the light gun established in the bows of the ship. The three crouched on the deck said nothing, but Joey had had time to see a little lugger sinking lower in the water, and guessed that she had been hit. Her crew had got away in their one dinghy, and were pulling with all their might towards the yacht. As she knelt there, hugging the shrieking baby to her, Joey breathed a brief prayer that the men might be saved. Then there came a crash which made the vessel heel over, followed by another, and at the same time she was aware of tremendous splashes which sent the water over the deck and drenched them all. She was so anxious over trying to keep her baby dry that it was not till some time after that she realized that the crashes came from Nigel's own gun, while the splashes were caused by bombs dropped from a German biplane which had just come up.

Almost at once, there came a terrific droning of engines, followed by the rat-tat-tat-tat of machine-gun fire. Immediately Nigel was at them again, this time urging them back to the shelter of the cabin. Clutching the wailing babies, they got back somehow, and then followed such an experience as the three grown-ups never forgot.

CHAPTER 3

War at First-Hand

The *Sea Witch* scarcely paused—scarcely waited long enough to pick up the boatload of men from the sunken lugger. The German plane was already swooping down to machine-gun the yacht, and Nigel Willoughby, with thoughts of the women and babies aboard, gave little heed to the sailors. With the seamanship learned through many years of pleasure yachting, he swung his wheel over, bringing the vessel round, almost in a circle, and so missing a bomb which fell within twenty yards of the *Sea Witch*. Almost at the same time the raider opened fire with his machine gun; but already the British fighter was on to him, and he had to turn to defend himself. In the meantime, the men from the lugger had pulled alongside and, abandoning their boat, were swinging themselves up on to the yacht like so many monkeys. There were only four of them, so it was speedily done.

"This is awful!" almost sobbed Frieda, sitting in a crouching position, little Connie held close to her. "Oh, shall we ever get safely to England?"

No one answered her. Joey was engaged in soothing Margot, who seemed likely to scream herself into a fit; while Bill, *her* charge having subsided to a low whimpering, sat with her eyes fixed on as much as she could see of the air-battle from the porthole.

Nigel had issued his orders below. The yacht was an oil-fed steam-yacht, and he had used sails in the first instance in the hope that they might more easily escape the attentions of any enemy plane who would be more likely to trouble over a steamship than a sailing vessel. This had proved fruitless, so he had signalled down to the engine room, where he had taken the precaution of keeping up a low pressure of steam, and already the engines were moving and giving greater impetus to the boat.

The *Sea Witch* drew off from the scene of the battle; but fresh reinforcements were coming up for the German. A bomber—one of the new, fast bombers—had picked up the noise of the gunfire and was hastening to join in the battle. They heard the deep, guttural coughing of her engines as she approached the spot, and then there came a terrific splash and the boat heeled over till the water raced over her counter. It was almost touch and go; but the *Sea Witch* was built for hard service as well as for pleasure. She had come from a famous Hampshire yacht-building yard, and she weathered it. She righted herself, the water streaming off her, and Nigel, putting his helm hard over, signalled desperately for every pound of steam his engineer could contrive to give him, and set his course due west.

The bomber might have tried again, but her sister was already badly damaged, and the British fighter was pressing her hard. The Germans gave up the easier prey, and opened fire on the fighter. The first German plane was losing height rapidly, and already it seemed unlikely that she could reach home. She barked a last discharge at her opponent, and received her death sentence as a burst of machine-gun fire set her petrol tank ablaze. Two figures, one in flames, dropped from her to take their chance with the sea, and the British turned to face their new foe, even as the Germans left their burning plane.

Nigel was unable to help. Gritting his teeth at the thought of his helplessness, he gave his full attention to getting away with his precious freight, his only comfort being the knowledge that at least he had saved four British lives and had managed to damage the U-boat, so that, judging by what he had seen, she was unable to submerge. With any luck she would be caught, and her men taken prisoner.

"And it's a long way more good luck than good management!" he thought to himself. "Confound my eyesight! And now I must take care."

He adjusted the glasses which he had been forced to assume three years previously, and put his whole heart into getting away. Twenty minutes later, he handed over to one

28

of the men, and went down to the cabin to find his passengers still sitting on the floor. The babies had cried themselves into a weary slumber; but Bill was looking very white, and so was Frieda. As for Jo, her cheeks were scarlet and her eyes brilliant. When he stooped to pat her hand, he was startled at its dry heat.

"All serene!" he said, speaking as casually as he could. "We've got away from that; and with luck, we'll have no further adventures. Jenks is bringing you people some tea, and mind you drink it. I'm using the steam-gear to get us there as fast as possible, so we oughtn't to be long now. Keep your chins up!"

He left the cabin after that, and Bill and Frieda relaxed a little. Not so Joey. She had suffered a good deal over having to leave her home, and she had run a temperature very easily all her life. Extremely delicate as a little child, her years in the Tyrol had done much for her. But robust she would never be, and with her excitable temperament and vivid imagination she would keep her tendency to fever as long as she lived. Bill knew this, and was thankful for the steaming tea which arrived a few minutes later. She made the girl drink it, and then got her to lie down on one of the seats that ran round the cabin. Little Margot was handed over to Frieda, and Bill issued a stern command to Jo against any talk.

"You hold your tongue and lie still," she said severely. "Do you want to be ill and upset the children? Then be quiet."

Jo obeyed. She was really feeling too poorly to argue. Her head seemed to be swollen to an enormous size, and yet to be so light that if it were not attached to her shoulders, she knew it would float away.

"And a nice sight I'd look then!" she thought.

By this time they were beyond the noise of the air-battle, and the only sounds that came to the women in the cabin were the footsteps of the men on deck, the gurgle and whisper as the keel of the vessel cut through the waters, and the steady throb-throb-throb of the engines. Nigel was crowding on every ounce of pressure that could be got. He knew that even an extra pound might make all the difference. For if the German bomber succeeded in shaking off her enemy, she would surely come in search of her prey once more. And this was not the Channel of former days, with its crowds of shipping everywhere.

"Let's hope Nigel doesn't make a mistake and hit the coast somewhere," thought Bill drowsily, as she sat beside Joey, watching her anxiously. "That *would* complicate matters. I wonder if the other folk had such adventures when they crossed. And yet I might have known how it would be. Joey is a regular fly-paper where adventures are concerned, and always was. But oh! I do hope this is going to be the last time we have to move until we can get back, either to Guernsey or to the Tyrol."

Nigel himself appeared in the doorway as she reached this point, and beckoned to her. "Will you come, Miss Wilson? I want a word."

Bill got up and stretched herself and followed him out of the cabin to the deck. She glanced round and saw, to her surprise, that a menacing grey shape lay not far off. They were hove-to, though so drowsy had she been that she had never noticed the cessation of the motion, and a small boat was putting off from the destroyer and pulling towards them.

"She signalled us to stop," explained Nigel. "I suppose, really, we are breaking all sorts of laws. What I want to know is how Joey is?"

"Feverish. I made her lie down and keep quiet. But I'll be thankful to get her ashore and into a doctor's hands. She's had a good deal of strain, one way and another, lately; and she really was ill after we escaped from the Tyrol. I know Jack Maynard was very anxious about her for a month or two. I'm making her keep quiet, and as soon as we reach safety she must go to bed. It won't do for her to be upset. There are the triplets to think of as well, you know."

"All right. You go back to them and I'll do the interviewing. That's all I wanted to know."

Nigel went to the counter of the yacht to welcome his visitors, and Bill returned to the cabin where the rest and the enforced quiet were at last beginning to have their effect on Joey. The brilliant flush was paler, and she was in her right mind instead of muttering rapidly as she had done for an hour or two. Bill bent over her and moistened her lips with a little water. Then she laid her down again.

"What did Nigel want?" asked the patient weakly.

"Just to tell me that the Navy has got to us, so we are fairly safe now," replied Bill calmly. "You shut your eyes and get a nap before we go ashore. The babies are all right. Frieda and I gave them bottles an hour ago, and they're sleeping peacefully. You follow their example."

Joey smiled and closed her eyes. She roused up half an hour later when a big man in naval uniform, with the rings of a surgeon-commander on the sleeve of his monkey jacket, came in and stooped over her.

"Hello!" she said—still weakly, though there was more life in her voice than there had been last time.

"Well, Mrs Maynard," said the visitor. "I hear you're not quite fit after all the excitement you've had. Let me see. Ah! H'm! Now put this under your tongue, and don't chew it. Are these the triplets I've been hearing about? Jolly youngsters, and healthy without a doubt. My name is Wynne, by the way. Now let me have that thing." He removed the thermometer from her lips and studied it. "Yes, you're up a point or two," he said, rinsing it in the glass of water Bill gave him. "The sooner you people get to land and a decent bed the better. We're going to take you there. We're hoping to make port in an hour or so, so we're taking you all off, and Mr Willoughby can take his own time about following. Give me the rug, please." Frieda handed him the big rug, and he carefully swathed Joey in it after he had first removed her lifebelt. Then he swung her up in his arms, carried her on to deck, and in three minutes more she was in the boat, and Bill was sitting beside her, while Frieda followed with the babies.

"Goodbye!" yelled Nigel, leaning over the rail. "See you folk some time soon, I hope."

31

Jo roused herself. "Goodbye, Nigel, old thing. Many thanks for all you've done. I'll write to Rosamund later."

Then the men pulled away from the yacht, and she drowsed off in Bill's arms. When she came to herself again she was in a quiet room with a low, raftered ceiling, and muslin curtains drifting back and forth from latticed windows. Frieda sat beside her, and from a big, wooden cradle in the corner came a cosy, purring sound. Someone had undressed her, for she was in a nightdress, and her hair was tumbling over the snowy pillows in two long plaits. She made a little sound, and at once the purring noise stopped, and the fattest woman she had ever seen heaved herself up from her knees by the cradle and bundled across the room to her.

"There now, my dear, do yu lay quiet, and yu'm sune be vit."

"Where—where is this?" demanded Joey. Her head felt its normal size again, and though she was weak, she was almost herself.

"It's Devonshire, Joey," said Frieda, leaning over her. "This is Mrs Laynard. This is the village inn, and the triplets are safe and asleep in the cradle over there. They've had bottles just a little time ago, and are quite fit and well."

"What time is it?"

"Taime vor you to have some broth, my dear." And Mrs Laynard got herself out of the room as fast as her bulk would allow her.

Frieda, left to tell the news, told it gently. The destroyer had brought them swiftly to England, landed them, and Joey, still sunk in the half-stupor which had ensued when she was safe aboard the big ship, had been carried to this inn, where she had lain for two days and one night. A wire had come from Nigel to say that he had reached his own port safely, but the *Sea Witch*, as they learned later, was commandeered by the Navy, and loud and long did its owner curse that his eyesight prevented him from going with her. But of service there could be no hope for him for many months to come. A cataract was forming over one eye, and he must wait till it was ripe for removal.

Commander Wynne had assured them that a few days in bed would be all Joey would need to put her right, but she must stop feeding her babies herself at once. She rebelled against this, but gave in when she found that nursing even one of them would make her unfit for anything, even if the child profited by it, which was doubtful.

"And they do look sweet with cups and spoons," added Frieda. "They are getting big girls now, Joey—nearly six months. And, luckily, they haven't hurt a bit. Now, here comes Mrs Laynard with your broth, and then you must go to sleep again. You'll be quite well in a few days."

And so, Joey found, she was. A week to that day, they were all able to say goodbye to good Mrs Laynard, and set out by slow train for the junction, whence they could catch another train to Exeter, and so to Armiford, where Madge was waiting for them, having written to say that her own house was more or less in order, and she had done what she could for Joey's, which was only a few doors away.

As for the school, a letter from Miss Annersley informed Bill that, after the hair-raising experiences of the advance-guard, they had decided to move as speedily as possible, and before another week was over Mr Howell had told them that Plas Howell was ready for them at once, and nothing was to be gained by delaying the removal.

"Well, here begins another chapter," said Jo as the train moved slowly out of the station. "Heaven send it's a more peaceful one than the last!"

"Amen to that!" agreed Bill.

But none of them yet realized what lay before England in the coming months, nor how highly her mettle was to be tried.

CHAPTER 4

At the School

"Penny for them, Robin!"

Robin Humphries turned round from the window where she had been standing, staring unseeingly at the spring beauty of the garden, and her face relaxed in a smile. "I'm afraid they're not worth it, Polly. I was only wondering how Joey and the rest are getting on in England."

Polly Heriot, a prefect who would leave school at the end of the summer term, and who was, therefore, almost grown-up, since she had just celebrated her eighteenth birthday, laid an arm round the slim shoulders of the younger girl. "So do we all. But at least we know that they are safely there. That's something. What I wonder is what sort of a crossing they had. We've heard nothing so far."

"It was only a wire from Bill," Robin pointed out. "You couldn't say much in a wire."

" 'Arrived safely. All well'," quoted Polly. "It doesn't tell you much, does it? However, they've been there a week now, so we ought to be getting letters any day. And Mrs Chester and Barbara have reached the Ozannes safely, too. Do you know what the Eltringhams are going to do?"

"The children—that is Nita and the boys—are to go to Mrs Eltringham's people. But she is staying here, and so is the baby, of course."

"I wonder if there's really any need for all this?" mused Polly.

"I wonder that myself," put in a fresh voice with more than a hint of an American accent. "Poppa said nothing last week when he was over."

Polly and Robin turned to welcome the Head Girl of the school, Cornelia Flower, a short, rather stocky young person of Polly's age, whose most noticeable features were a pair of vividly blue eyes of enormous size, bright, fair hair, and an amazingly square jaw. She wore glasses as the result of an accident in the previous autumn, and her hair was closely cropped for the same reason. No one could have called her pretty, and indeed she would have hooted loudly at the idea, but hers was a face that always drew a second glance. She, Polly, the Robin, and Daisy Venables were the only girls at the school at present, for the Easter holidays had begun two days ago. But Cornelia's father was a busy man, and, as she was motherless, there was no home for her. The school had taken its place for the past six years. Polly Heriot was an orphan, whose guardian was a solicitor in a quiet little country town in the home counties, and he had flatly refused to have the girl there in case of any air raids. Polly had raged at the dictum at first, for she was very fond of old Mr. Wilmot, who was a lonely man now, since his sister had died the previous year at the mature age of eighty-seven. However, rage as she might, it did no good, for he was quite firm about it, so she had to put up with it as best she might. At least, she would have Cornelia, who was a chum of hers; and Robin and Daisy were there as well.

Now she laughed, and pulled the Head Girl into a chair nearby. "You sit there, Corney Flower, and don't try to do too much. What do you expect will be our job after lunch?"

"We've got to finish packing the books," replied Cornelia. "I guess that'll take us up till tea-time. Where's Daisy, Robin? I've seen nothing of her all morning."

"She went to help Nally with the gym things," said Robin, perching herself on the windowsill. "We must work hard, you know. The men are coming tomorrow to take the furniture. Oh dear!" she went on, "what a dreadful business it all is! Our dear school moved again!"

"Wish I could see Hitler alone for half an hour!" Cornelia sounded savage. "Guess I'd make him sorry for himself all right."

"I've heard that when he is angry he chews the chair legs," said Polly thoughtfully. "I should imagine the furniture would suffer if you really got going with him, Corney."

Cornelia, who in earlier years had been famed for her startling vocabulary, grinned at this. "I guess it would. I know I talk like an *Elsie* book these days, but I haven't forgotten anything and I'd make him sit up all right, I'll tell the world."

"I'm sure you would," agreed Polly pensively. "The bother is I don't believe he understands English, and the worst things you could say wouldn't sound so bad in German."

"Oh, I know a fair amount of German, too," retorted Cornelia with a chuckle. "And some of it isn't—well—parliamentary."

The other two joined in her chuckles. It was always fairly safe to say that Cornelia's flow of language would shock proper people on occasion, whether it were English, French, or German; and, like all members of the Chalet School, she was practically trilingual.

Ten years before this, Mrs Russell, then Madge Bettany, and Mademoiselle Lepâttre had established the Chalet School on the shores of the Tiernsee, loveliest of Austria's many lovely lakes. Four years later, Madge had married Dr Russell, head of the great Sanatorium on the Sonnalpe at the far side of the lake. Mademoiselle had remained as managing Head, and had carried it on as they had planned. Then the rape of Austria had meant, first, the flight of Joey, Miss Wilson, Robin, and two or three other people who had aroused the anger of the Gestapo; and later, the removal of the school to Guernsey where they had been for two terms only. Now they had to go again, since there seemed to be some danger of air raids. Mercifully, Mademoiselle, who had been in bad health for the past three years, had died in the autumn, so would know nothing of all this. Miss Annersley, who had been appointed as Principal since Mademoiselle's breakdown, would continue as they had begun.

"There's one thing," said Polly. "Jo and the others are there already, so they will be able to make preparations for us. I wonder what Plas Howell is like? Miss Annersley

36

showed me some photos last night, and it looks all right from the outside—a huge place. But we have to live *inside*. If the rooms are tiny and dozens of them, it won't be such fun.''

"There's Charlie calling," said Robin, dropping to the floor from the windowsill. "Come! We had best not keep her waiting. She is so easy to annoy just now."

"Yes, hasn't she got a temper!" commented Cornelia, following them from the room. "Guess something's up with her. She's got her rag out all the time. Maybe, though, it's because of the bother of having to move school," she added charitably. "That sure is a nuisance, however you look at it."

By this time they had reached the door of what had been the library, where pretty Miss Stewart, a shadow on her face, was wrestling with the piles of books and big packing-cases lying about.

"Come along, girls!" she said irritably, as the three entered. "What have you been doing? All these books must be packed before tea, and how you think it's going to be done if you idle your time away as you seem to be doing, I don't know. Robin—no; you, Cornelia—bring these volumes of the Encyclopaedia and lay them in the bottom of this case. Robin, you can pack the poets into this one. Polly, help Cornelia. And where is Daisy?''

"She's in the gym, helping Miss Nalder," said Robin as she began her work. "Do you want her, Miss Stewart?"

"Not if she's occupied properly," snapped Miss Stewart, rapidly fitting volumes of history into a third case. "But please remember that the men come tomorrow, and all these cases must be nailed and roped before then. Yes, what is it, Michelle?''

"A gentleman to see you, Miss. I have put him in the drawing-room," replied Michelle.

"Very well, I'll come. Girls, go on with your work; and remember—I want to see at least four cases ready if I'm away more than a few minutes." And with these words, the mistress went off to interview her visitor, leaving the girls looking at each other.

"She's worse than usual," said Polly, who had not ceased to bring the volumes for Cornelia to pack. "I wonder what's up with her?"

"Perhaps she has toothache," suggested Robin from the bookshelves, where she was selecting the largest books to put on the floor of the case.

"I saw no signs of it." Polly sounded disgruntled. "If you ask me the only pain she's got is in her temper."

"Oh, well, I guess she'll get over it once we've got safely to England," said Cornelia easily. "You buck up with those books and let's get one case done, anyway. I guess they'll most fill this box, won't they?"

The three worked hard, and case after case was filled and left ready for the men to nail up and rope, and still Miss Stewart did not return. The warning bell for lunch rang, and they had to leave their labours, and go to tidy themselves. Lunch was served, and they, Daisy Venables, Miss Nalder, Miss Annersley, and Simone Lecoutier had it comfortably, and there was no sign of the history mistress. None of the staff made any comments on her absence, so the girls could not, and were left wondering what had happened. After lunch, the Head came to see how they were progressing, and complimented them on what they had done.

"Finish, if you can," she said. "You need do nothing more after that. You have worked splendidly, girls."

"When do we cross, Miss Annersley?" asked Polly.

"In two days' time, I hope," replied the Head. "Simone, are you staying to help them? Very well, dear. I think there is nothing else you can do at present."

Simone Lecoutier, an old girl of the school, and well known to both Robin, Daisy, and Cornelia in that capacity, though Polly had known her only as a mistress, nodded, and laughed, and joined the quartet in helping to pack the books. It was a long job, for the Chalet School boasted an excellent library, and everything was to go.

"I wonder who Charlie's visitor was?" said Cornelia, halfway through the afternoon, when twelve big cases had

38

been finished, and they were busy with the next two. "No one seems to have seen anything of her since he came. I hope there's nothing wrong—bad news from home, or something like that."

Simone looked at her, and began to laugh. Cornelia was down on her in a moment. "Say, Simone, if you know and it's all that funny, you're real mean if you don't share the joke. I guess we all need something to cheer us up a mite, anyhow. Spill the beans—come on, now!"

"It's a good thing for you, Corney, that this isn't term-time," retorted Simone. "As for Charlie's visitor, I thought you'd been told."

"Not a word," said Robin. "Who is it, Simone?"

"Her fiancé, of course."

"Her—*what?*"

"Her fiancé—Mr Mackenzie from Singapore. Did you not know, then?"

"Gee! What d'you know about that?" demanded Cornelia, appealing to the world at large. "Say, Simone, is *that* what's been wrong with Charlie? We thought she'd got a pain in her temper."

"Charlie's wedding has been put off twice, as you know," returned Simone, very busy with geography readers belonging to the Juniors. "It should have taken place this spring, but when war broke out, Mr Mackenzie was unable to leave Singapore; and, of course, she could not go to him. So it has made her very unhappy."

Cornelia, who possessed as much sentiment as a suitcase, murmured, "It's made her real bad-tempered, anyway. I guess if that's what being in love does for you, I'll keep clear of it."

"But if he could not come, how has he come now?" demanded Robin.

"He was sent home on business for his firm. He has come to bring her back with him—no; I mean *take* her back with him," Simone corrected herself, for though her English was mostly fluent she still used constructions that helped to remind her friends that she was French.

"Do you mean she won't come back to school?" Daisy sounded aghast. "But—how awful! Why, Charlie is *part* of the school."

Simone laughed. "When he has come to take her with him and to marry her? No, ma belle; she will not return to the school to teach. But I must say no more. Instead, let us finish these last two cases, and then we will go out into the garden and pluck flowers to take to the Sanatorium tomorrow when we go to make our farewells."

However, they were fated not to carry out this eminently sensible plan. Just as Simone fitted in the last of the books, and Robin and Polly were looking round the denuded shelves to make sure that nothing had been overlooked, Michelle again appeared at the door to say that Miss Annersley wished to see Mademoiselle Lecoutier. Simone got up off her knees, dusting her hands together, and giving the rapid little touches to her attire that always kept her as neat as a new pin.

"I will come, Michelle. Did Miss Annersley say if she wished me to bring anything? No? Then go and tidy yourselves, you four, and go into the gar—"

So far she got, when there came the sound of flying footsteps down the corridor. The next moment, Michelle was shoved unceremoniously on one side, and a slight, incredibly chic damsel flung herself on Simone with staccato ejaculations and endearments in French.

After the first gasp, Simone returned the caresses and endearments as wholeheartedly as they were given, and the four girls looked round hastily for some means of retreat, since the mistress and her visitor occupied the doorway. It was left to Cornelia to recognize the latter.

"Renée!" she cried. "Renée Lecoutier! I thought you were in Paris. What under the canopy brings you here?"

Renée, with a last hug and double kiss, released Simone, and advanced to administer the same to the Head Girl. "Corney! But what then—Ah! I remember! Simone told me of your accident with those crapauds!" She clenched her fists, and gritted her little white teeth together on the last word. "Were your eyes much harmed, my Corney?"

"No, but I've got to wear these a year or two. You never mind me, but tell us why you've come just when we're going."

"Papa and Maman feared—oh, I do not know what. So, as the dear Cousine Thérèse was gone, we just packed those souvenirs we valued, and came here, first, to see Simone. Then we go to England. And it is possible that we may go later to your own great country, Corney. Ah, Robin! How long it is since I have seen you!" And she fell on Robin, with whom she had been great friends in their early schooldays. Renée had left school at fifteen to go to the Paris Conservatoire of Music, and she and Robin had not met since then, so the meeting between them was one of great joy on both sides. Meanwhile, Simone, with a quick word or two to Polly and Daisy, had left the room to seek Miss Annersley and her own parents.

"We are coming with you!" announced Renée presently. "Maman will be—how do you say it?—housekeeper—for the school, and attend to les affaires; and Papa will do all his possible in whatever way he is needed until we decide if we go to America or not. Come, all of you. For I hear Simone calling, and Papa and Maman will wish to see you. Oh, but I am glad to be with you again! How glad, I cannot say!"

CHAPTER 5

Gwensi

Meanwhile, while the school was busy getting ready to leave the happy island where they had first found refuge from the Germans, in a big mansion in Armishire, close to the borders of South Wales, a small girl of thirteen was wandering about, looking at everything with mournful eyes that seemed to be bidding everything goodbye. Gwensi Howell felt as if the bottom had dropped out of her world, more especially since her adored stepbrother Ernest had said goodbye to her that morning and departed to join his ship.

For the past nine years of her life she had been the pet and plaything of Ernest and his old godfather, and only the fact that she had had a very sane daily governess who had insisted on obedience and a certain amount of self-control had saved her from becoming a thoroughly spoilt child. Now old Mr Howell had gone, and Ernest had left her, and the home which had been hers for nine years was to be turned into a school. Gwensi hated it all, and felt that, for two pins, she could have flung herself down on the floor and kicked and screamed as she had often done in her baby days.

To her came Megan, her old nurse, who was staying on to help the new housekeeper—a Frenchwoman, so they had been told, and mother of one of the mistresses. Megan had taken a big hand in the spoiling of her baby, and she was grieved now when she saw the sulky little face under the shadow of the ripples of silky black hair that framed the small, pointed face, and hung over her shoulders in two long pigtails.

"Cariad," she began, but Gwensi flung away at once from her.

"Go away, Megan! I don't want you—I want nobody!"

Megan looked at her, then turned away in silence. What Gwensi Howell really needed at this time was a good spanking but there was no one with the authority to do it. So she went on wandering about, making herself thoroughly miserable, and thinking that never had any girl been so unhappy or so badly treated before.

Finally she fetched up in the library where she had spent so many happy hours with her brother, flopped down on one of the broad window seats, and gazed out of the window with such a wretched little face that anyone seeing it would have imagined that she was utterly destitute and alone in the world.

"I think it was horrid of Ernest to bring a horrid school here!" she told a thrush who was hopping about on the lawn outside. "As though the war wasn't horrid enough without all that!"

"Three 'horrids' in two sentences. Isn't that two too many?" demanded a voice from the doorway.

Gwensi jumped at the unexpected remark, and turned round to face the tall, dark girl who was standing there with an air of being in her rightful place.

"What—who are you?" she stammered.

"Me? I'm Mrs Maynard—Joey Maynard," replied the owner of the name. "Mrs Russell's sister," she added, kindly taking pity on the bewildered expression in the child's face. "I've come over to see that everything is all right for the school—or as much of it as should be arriving before long. Mercy on us, child! What's the matter?" For Gwensi had suddenly leapt to her feet, and was standing facing her with flaming eyes, scarlet cheeks, and a general appearance of being about to fly at her.

"You belong to that *horrid* school? And you walk in here as if you owned the place! I hate you—I hate you all! Do you hear me?"

Jo Maynard grinned irrepressibly. "I should think they must hear you down in the village! No need to yell, I'm not deaf. Then you must be Mr Howell's young sister—Gwensi, isn't it?"

"My name's Guenever," said the owner of the name sullenly.

43

"I've heard of you." Jo's tone was pleasantly interested, and Gwensi, brought up short in her diatribe, eyed her doubtfully.

Jo crossed the room to the chair before the big desk and sat down so that she was more on a level with the child. She looked at her thoughtfully. She saw a slight child, with a pair of big dark eyes set in a small face. At present the sensitive mouth was set in a straight, sulky line, but Jo had an idea that when things were going well with Gwensi Howell she had a pretty smile. The little nose was slightly tilted, and the skin was clear and creamy, with cheeks which, at present, were blazing with the fury that was surging up in the small girl.

"*Why* do you call the school 'horrid'?" demanded Jo, as Gwensi seemed to have nothing further to say at the moment.

"Because it is!"

"That's no answer. Haven't you been taught to argue properly?"

Before Gwensi could reply, a funny little cry brought Mrs Maynard to her feet. "That's Margot! Come and see my babies. I'll bet you've never seen triplets before. I've got them outside on the lawn in their pram. I thought they were asleep and would stay so, but that was a mistake—one I'm often making, though I've had six months to get accustomed to them now, and you'd think I'd know better after six months, wouldn't you?" She grinned infectiously, and, despite herself, Gwensi felt her scowl relaxing. She followed the lady out of the room, rather wondering at herself for doing so. Also, she rather wondered at this treatment. Hitherto, people had either grieved openly at her tempers, or left her to them. This calm ignoring of them and bringing up a fresh subject was something quite new to her. Besides, she had heard from Megan about Mrs Maynard and her red-headed triplets, and was secretly curious to see them. So she followed Jo meekly from the room, down the big hall, and out into the sunshiny garden where daffodils, national flower of Wales, nodded golden heads in the fresh breeze.

44

Jo turned to the right, and led the way over the grass to where, outside a French window, stood a big pram from which issued the wails that had caught her quick ear.

"Bad girl!" she scolded in tender tones as she bent over it, and lifted out the baby. "Didn't Mamma tell you you were all to be good and quiet while she was gone? What's all this about?" She turned to Gwensi laughingly. "Come and see them, Gwensi. Margot's wakened her sisters with her howls, of course. She's always the one to begin. The other two are good as gold that way, though Len is a fearful wriggler. Here, would you like to hold one of them?"

She tucked the indignant Margot under one arm and lifted out another of the babies, and deposited her in Gwensi's arms. "That's Connie, the best-behaved of the three. Her eyes are rather lovely, aren't they?"

Clutching the small thing to her, Gwensi looked down into the brown depths that were lifted to her face. The scowl had quite vanished now, and dimples dipped into the cheeks which had lost their angry flush.

"Oh! Isn't she *pretty*!" she exclaimed, as Jo lifted Margot to her shoulder, and began patting the tiny back expertly. "I never saw such a pretty baby before! What beautiful eyes! And are they all alike?"

Secretly well pleased at the result of her manoeuvres, Jo laughed. "No—thank Heaven! I shouldn't know them apart if they were. Len's are grey—like wood violets. And Margot's—when she's finished screwing them up—you will see are blue. My husband is very fair—as fair as I am dark. Hence the different colours of the eyes. There, Babykin! Is that better? It was just a little wind, wasn't it? Mamma has put it right now, though."

Gwensi looked up at her. "Are they to call you that? It does sound so funny and old-fashioned!"

Rocking the now comforted Margot in her arms, Joey nodded. "I know. But 'Father' and 'Mother' are difficult for very tiny people to get hold of, and I'm tired of 'Daddy' and 'Mummy', so Jack—that's my husband—and I thought we'd start a new fashion. Besides," she added with a chuckle, "I knew it would create a minor sensation—and it did!"

Involuntarily, Gwensi joined in the chuckle. Then, still holding Connie carefully, she turned to the pram. "May I see the other one? What did you call her?"

"Len. Actually, Mary Helena. She's named after a great friend of mine who is also her godmother. The one you have is named Mary Constance after *her* godmother, who is another friend. And my babiest daughter is Mary Margaret after my brother-in-law's sister. We did it to please her own elder girl, Daisy. Margot died little more than a year ago, and Daisy has grieved bitterly. So when our triplets came, we decided to call the littlest one Margot too. It's helped Daisy, I think. By the way, she must be about your age, I think. Thirteen, aren't you? When are you fourteen?"

"I was thirteen last month," explained Gwensi shyly.

"March? Why, Daisy's birthday is then, too! What date? The fourteenth? Bless me! Then you two are twins—of a sort."

All her hatred of the school forgotten in these new interests that were crowding on her, Gwensi looked up eagerly. "Really? And is she coming here?"

"Well, of course. She and my Robin are going to live with me at Plas Gwyn, but they're coming to school, of course. It's rather a long way away—three miles, even with bicycles," said Jo rather incoherently, "but they've always lived with me since we were married, and I couldn't do without them. Look here, Gwensi, I've got to go now; but I'll be up this afternoon to welcome Miss Annersley and the other people who are coming with her, and I'll introduce you to Daisy then. You certainly must know her. And there's her chum, Beth Chester, too. Bethy is the same age as you two. You'll have to make triplets among you!" She laughed again, and Gwensi smiled shyly in response. "Walk with me a little way down the drive," went on this unexpected person. "Wait a moment till I pop Margot into the pram. Would you like to wheel it a little when I've got it off the grass? Come along then."

Gwensi was charmed to wheel the big pram down the gravelled drive. She had had very little to do with babies. Her stepbrother had been too much afraid of infection to allow her to have much to do with the cottage folk at Howell Village, and there were few families of children near them. Those that there were happened to be either her own age or older; so this was almost the first time she had held a baby in her arms, and certainly the first time she had ever been trusted to wheel any pram.

Joey walked by her side, keeping an eye on her. She did not think that the child would upset the babies, but it was as well to be careful. The small people were blooming in the sweet, fresh air from the Welsh mountains; even Margot, the youngest, who was also the frailest, was making marked progress. But an accident would be good for no one, and Gwensi was plainly inexperienced. The small girl took them to the lodge gates where Jo took over with a nod, and a cheery "Goodbye! See you this afternoon."

"Will you bring the babies with you?" asked Gwensi breathlessly.

Jo shook her head. "Not this afternoon. They must stay at home and have their nap. Besides, I don't want to walk so far. It's two and a half miles to our home, and that makes five miles of pram-pushing already today. I'll come in the car with my sister, I expect. But Saturday is a holiday, and I'll ask Miss Annersley if you may come with Daisy and Robin to spend the day. I *think* we shall have got all our gossiping finished by that time!" she added with another laugh. Then she turned down the road, pushing the pram before her, and Gwensi watched her out of sight before turning to go up the broad drive to seek her dinner.

As she ate her cold chicken and fresh greens from the garden, the small girl meditated on this strange new friend of hers. She felt that Mrs Maynard *was* a friend, even though they had just met. Perhaps, she mused, the school people would be a little like her. It mightn't be quite so bad then. Then she remembered that it also meant that the house would be given over to strangers. She would no

47

longer be able to go about as she chose. The rooms that had been her own private hunting-grounds would be so no longer. Ernest had told her the night before he went away that the library would be Miss Annersley's private room, and she must not expect to go trotting in and out as she had done previously. The big drawing-room had been cleared and was to be the school hall; and the small one, opening out of it, would be the staff room. All that would be left to her would be her own little bedroom, which had been the dressing-room opening out of her brother's. She had pleaded so hard that she might still retain it, and not be in a dormitory with other girls, that he had written to Miss Annersley about it. That lady had agreed, telling him in her letter that she expected that by the end of the first term his little sister would be clamouring to be with other girls of her own age; but she quite agreed with him that it would be as well not to plunge the child into too many new experiences at once. So Gwensi was to keep her forget-me-not room, with all its dainty appointments.

She got up from the table, completely ignoring the pudding Megan had made especially for her darling, and rushed off to it, to shut herself in, fling herself on the bed, regardless of the way she was crumpling the pretty counterpane, and cried stormily.

Megan found her there an hour later when she went in with a bowl of daffodils she had arranged for the table in the window. By that time Gwensi had cried herself to a standstill, and lay with the sobs catching her breath, and wet lashes; but the tears were ended. Good-hearted Megan caught the child to her breast, murmuring soothing Welsh endearments to her. She meant nothing but the best for the little girl but her treatment was most injudicious. By the time Gwensi was more or less calm, all the influence of Jo's matter-of-fact treatment had worn off, and the hatred Gwensi had fostered towards the school which was coming was uppermost in her heart.

Megan coaxed her to go and wash her tear-stained face, and change her skirt and jumper for a pretty frock. She brushed out the long, silky hair, and tied it back loosely from the sullen little face. Then she whipped off the crumpled counterpane, and produced a fresh one. By that time it was after three, and there was the sound of a car coming up the drive. Gwensi went to the window which was over the door, and looked out. It contained Mrs Maynard; a smaller, older lady whom she knew to be Mrs Russell, the owner of the school; a slender woman, obviously older than either, whom she guessed to be Miss Annersley, the administrative Head; and someone still older, very small and wiry-looking, whom she could not place at all.

An ugly scowl came over the small, irregular face, and then Gwensi drew back hurriedly, and hid behind the forget-me-not blue curtains, for Jo Maynard was looking up as if seeking along the windows for her.

"She belongs to Them! I hate Them! I must hate her, too!" thought the small rebel. She looked round the room which Megan had quitted a minute before. Her hat and coat lay on the bed. It was the work of a moment to snatch them up, and then Gwensi was slipping along the corridor, down the backstairs, through the kitchen where she stayed long enough to snatch up a couple of apples and some bread-and-butter, and so out through the kitchen garden, and up the orchard to her own little hidey-hole in the old yew-hedge which was two hundred years old and four feet thick. Years ago, Gwensi had discovered that, by dint of pushing and squeezing, she could get through a certain part, and creep along where, by some freak, the trees formed a hollow tunnel. Here, she had often hidden when at war with her world, and no one, so far, had discovered it. She determined to stay here for the present at any rate. Let them call! *She* wouldn't answer, if they called till they were black in the face! She hated the lot of them, and she'd show them that she didn't mean to be friends with any of them!

CHAPTER 6

Where is Gwensi?

"Well?" Joey Bettany, a pink flush in her cheeks, was looking anxiously at Miss Annersley, who stood beside the car, taking in the outlines of Plas Howell with critical eyes. "Do you like it?"

The quiet, grey eyes lit up with a charming smile as the Head nodded. "I do indeed. What a beautiful place! There will be plenty of room for our girls here. And what glorious air!" She sniffed appreciatively.

"Straight from the hills." Jo sounded rather as though she were personally responsible for the air. "You've seen my infants. Don't you think the girls will bloom in this?"

"The best thing possible for them," agreed Miss Annersley. "And the grounds are lovely. That meadowland near the gates will be ideal for playing-fields, and Mr Howell has given me carte blanche to do as I like about that sort of thing. Well, let's go into the house. I'm really curious to see it after the description you wrote to me last week."

Joey laughed. "Dear me. I didn't know I'd been so enthusiastic. I had just a peep at the lower rooms with Mr Howell. He didn't exactly want us on the premises when his small sister was about. I gathered from him that she was taking the change very badly; and judging by what I heard myself this morning, he wasn't far out. She was cursing us all most liberally."

"Was she?" Madge Russell looked worried. "What did you say to her, Jo? I hope you didn't upset her further?"

"Keep cool, my dear? I introduced her to the triplets, and told her about Daisy and Beth Chester. She was quite interested, so I hope you will find her a little more forthcoming than she might otherwise have been. She loved the babies, anyhow."

Matron—she was the fourth member of the party—laughed. "So you are prepared to stand by the child. I know you, Jo!" Her sharp eyes dwelt lovingly on the delicate, sensitive face. Wild horses wouldn't have dragged it from Matron, but Jo was her darling. She had nursed her through one serious illness and various minor complaints in her schoolgirl days. She had scolded her for the good of her soul, and her criticisms had been unsparing at times. All the same "Matey", as all the girls called her, would have willingly laid down her life for Jo at any time.

Jo didn't see the look, for she was scanning the second tier of windows eagerly, hoping to see the little pale face with its frame of dark silky curls that she had brought from sulks to smiles such a few hours ago. As we know, Gwensi saw her, and hid, so her quest was in vain; and presently the four ladies entered the house and reached the big hall just as the small girl was slipping down the backstairs on her way to her eyrie.

Miss Annersley looked round the big hall with its great fireplace, the two marble statue groups glimmering in the shadows near the stairs, the wide settles, and big, gate-legged table with its huge bowl of golden daffodils in the centre, and her lips parted in a smile of real pleasure. "What a charming place! Have you any idea of its age, Jo?"

"It's not so very old—built towards the end of Anne's reign," said Jo, who, as a lover of history, could generally be relied on to pick up details of this kind. "This must be delightfully cool in summer, but I should think it's on the cold side in the winter. This is the drawing-room which is to be the Hall. They've cleared it of everything, and stored the furniture in one of the cellars. It's quite a decent size, isn't it?"

It was a big room, with four windows stretching almost from floor to ceiling, facing southwest, and getting all the sun possible. The walls were covered with an expensive-looking French wallpaper in satin stripes, at the sight of which Miss Annersley uttered an exclamation of dismay.

The floor was parquet, brought to a fine polish by generations of hard rubbing. At one end of the room stood a Broadwood grand piano, and a high desk of polished ebony stood near it. Otherwise, the room was empty, save for the two great fireplaces with their accompaniments of pierced steel fenders, dogs, and fire-irons.

"This way," said Jo, leading them up the room to a door behind the piano. "Here is the pink drawing-room—and the staff room. Isn't it *rosy*?" It had been redecorated when old Mr Howell's mother had come to Plas Howell as a bride in the 1860s, and the panels in the walls had been filled with heavy silk brocade over which rioted a pattern of roses and true-lovers' knots. The white wood furniture was upholstered to match, and curtains of the same material hung at the two windows. Originally, it must have been very bright and gay; but the years had faded the brocades to a tender old-rose, and the very dark green of the carpet toned it down. Watercolour seascapes hung on the walls, and there were bowls of flowering bulbs here and there. The mistresses' bookshelves, which had come over three days ago and were placed round the walls, struck rather an incongruous note, especially as they remained empty. But the room was a pretty, restful one, all the same, and the Head only voiced the general feelings of everyone when she said, "Well, the staff *will* be in clover here! I hope I've come off as well!"

"You've got the library," replied Jo, as she led the way across the hall to the great room facing east and north. "Here you are—and I hope you're satisfied."

One glance round the noble room with its built-in shelves laden with books, its comfortable saddle-bag chairs and sofa, its Chinese carpet in glowing blues and oranges which relieved its somewhat cold aspect, and its big, useful desk told Miss Annersley that she fared equally well with her staff.

"What a glorious room!" she exclaimed. "But after my little study at Tiernsee and in Guernsey, it seems almost too large. Are you sure this is the room Mr Howell meant, Jo?"

"Well, that's what he said when he showed me round,"

returned Jo. "Of course, if you don't like it, you can always change it." She shot a wicked glance at the Head, and that lady laughed.

"You never did improve with keeping, did you, Joey? Very well. I will establish myself here. Now what else have you to show us?"

Room by room, Joey led them round the ground floor, pointing out the form-room arrangement *she* thought suitable. The morning-room for the Fifth; a smaller room, which had been used as the estate office, for the Sixth; a breakfast room, which would do for the Fourth; and the big billiard room, now denuded of its table, which would be ideal for the Kindergarten.

"As for the upstairs rooms, I've never seen them," she remarked. "We'd better send for Gwensi to show us round. I'll ring, shall I?" She suited the action to the word, and presently Megan appeared and was bidden to send Miss Gwensi to Mrs Maynard.

Megan went off, but presently returned to say that Gwensi was not in the house. She offered to do the showing round herself, and led the way up the noble staircase to the great gallery which ran round three sides of the fine hall, and from which the upstairs rooms opened.

Here the quartet found rooms that would make delightful dormitories, as well as smaller ones which would do for the mistresses. Finally Megan showed her darling's dainty chamber, and the ladies exclaimed with delight at it. The walls were panelled as so many were, and into the panels had been let brocade powdered with forget-me-nots and here and there a touch of pink bladder campion. The curtains, cushions, and counterpane all matched it; and the carpet was blue of the same tone, but much deeper in shade. The furniture was white, besprinkled with sprays of forget-me-nots and campion. A tall, white bookcase stood against one wall, crammed with books of various kinds, and Miss Annersley called Jo with a mischievous smile, and pointed out the four gaily-jacketed books which bore, under the titles, the name of Josephine Bettany.

"Here you are, Joey; here's another fan of yours."

Jo went very red. "Don't talk rot, Hilda! Here's a whole shelf of Elsie Oxenham, and another of Dorita Fairlie Bruce and Winifred Darch. If the kid is a fan of anything, it's of school stories." All the same her eyes sparkled. Jo wouldn't have let wild horses drag the secret from her, but she *did* think it rather nice to see those four books side by side. *Cecily Holds the Fort, Patrol-Leader Nancy, Tessa in the Tyrol*, and the very last one, which had been published only a month before, *Gypsy Jocelyn*, a story of a girl and a caravan holiday.

"I think I must get going on the new one as soon as we've got the school settled down," she remarked. Megan had left the room, since it was the last on that floor, and she was beginning to feel anxious about Gwensi's prolonged absence.

"What is it to be this time, Jo?" demanded Matron.

"Another Guide story, my dear," Jo's cheeks had resumed their normal colour, but her eyes were brilliant. "I say, you people! I've just realized that in another eight or ten years the triplets will be reading my books, and I'll have to begin writing for them. I wonder what their taste in literature will be? Len will probably want adventure stories; she's by far the most daring of the three. I actually found her trying to crawl out of her cot the other day. Mercifully, the sides were up, so she couldn't get far. Still, I expect I'll have some hair-raising times with her when she finds her feet. Margot will probably like stories of bad little boys and girls. And I'm morally certain Connie will demand fairy stories. Those big eyes of hers are very dreamy at times."

"That's nothing to go by," Matron assured her. "Whenever I saw *you* with a dreamy look in your eyes, I waited in fear and trembling for the next piece of outrageous mischief you could invent."

Madge Russell and Miss Annersley burst into laughter at this sally, and Jo blushed again. "Oh, come, Matey! I wasn't as bad as all that!"

"Every bit as bad," retorted Matron ruthlessly. "Well,

we seem to have finished with this floor. Shall we move on and see the rest? It's a big house, and time's getting on.''

They left the little room and went down the corridor towards the staircase, where they were met by Megan who was looking troubled. She took them upstairs, and they saw another series of rooms, some of which were destined for more dormitories, while others would become practising rooms, stock rooms, store-places, and the ones in the south wing would be sick-rooms, since a heavy baize door shut them off from the rest of the house. Above these lay the attics where the maids were housed. Several were shut up since they were empty, though Megan produced all the keys.

After this, they went downstairs again, and out through the kitchen across the stable yard, and into the big stable where Ernest Howell had proposed they should fit up a gymnasium. Next door to it were other buildings which would do for laboratory, art room, and geography room. Most of the school furniture had already arrived and had been sorted into the various places. Miss Annersley saw at a glance that their work had been considerably lightened, but that, at the same time, it would take them all their time to be ready by the first week in May, when the school was due to re-open.

''It's really very satisfactory,'' said Madge when at length they were strolling round the side of the house to view the kitchen garden. ''By the way, Hilda, I had a letter this morning from a Dr Marilliar. He wishes to enter his daughter and two nieces here, since their own school is closing down. The Head is giving up, and the house in which the school was is to be pulled down to make way for a new Woolworth's. They live at Medbury, about eighteen miles from here, and would be weekly boarders. Here it is. I'll hand it over to you.'' And she produced a letter from her bag, and passed it over to the Head.

''Three new girls at one burst? What fun!'' exclaimed Jo eagerly. ''What are their names and ages, Hilda?''

''Monica Marilliar and Vicky and Alixe McNab,''

replied Miss Annersley, who was scanning the letter rapidly. "Monica is nearly sixteen, Vicky is seventeen, and Alixe is not quite fifteen. Vicky would be with us only a year—she wants to be a doctor, he says. Monica and Alixe we should keep longer than that, of course. I see, Madge, that he also hints that we may very likely get two or three other girls from the same source, and I had a letter from Mr Howell's locum on Monday, asking if his two girls might come to us."

"Cheers!" interposed Jo. "At this rate, it begins to look as if we might hope to grow once more. Eight or nine new girls this coming term would give us a very nice lift up."

"And, luckily, we are keeping nearly all our Guernsey pupils," added her sister. Then, at the sound of hurrying footsteps, she turned.

It was Megan who was bearing down on them, a scared look in her eyes. "What on earth is the matter?" demanded Jo.

"I cannot find Miss Gwensi!" gasped the maid. "I went to bring her for you sent for her, and it is naughty of her to be away when she knew that you were coming this afternoon. But she is always like this when things do not please her. She *always* runs away and hides, and no one knows where she goes. But it is bad of her, well aye; yes indeed."

"Silly child!" said Madge Russell tolerantly. "I suppose she really does resent our coming here. Well, we'd better see if we can find her, I suppose, since she's in your charge now, Hilda. Suppose we separate. You go round the shrubbery, and Matey can hunt in the flower garden. I'll try that bit of woodland, and Joey can hunt through the kitchen garden and the orchard. Megan, call the rest of the maids together, and look through the house. If anyone finds her, bring her back to the library, and keep her there till the rest return."

They agreed to do this, and parted company, and Joey presently found herself promenading between rows of early cabbages on the one hand, and winter lettuces on the other. As she went, she whistled cheerfully with a note as sweet and true as a blackbird's, and the small truant, crouched in her little cave in the yew-hedge, heard her, and wondered.

Presently, a golden call of "Gwensi—Gwen-si! Where are you?" reached her ears, and she huddled closer to the ground. She had already heard Megan calling her, but had remained obstinately dumb. It took a greater effort for her not to reply now, for Gwensi was as musical as most of her nation, and Jo's voice, sweet and clear, with something of the almost celestial beauty of a choirboy's, tugged at her heart. But Gwensi was proud. She couldn't bear to be brought home like a naughty truant. So she stayed where she was, and Jo, hunt as she might, never caught the smallest glimpse of her. In the end, young Mrs Maynard had to return to her fellow-searchers and confess that she had been as unlucky as they. She had seen, to quote her own expressive phrase, "neither hair nor hide of the child."

"But this won't do!" exclaimed Miss Annersley worriedly. "I am in charge of her, and I *must* know where she is."

"Of course you must," agreed Matron, taking a hand. "Megan, have you *no* idea where the child can be?"

But Megan was as ignorant as they, and when six o'clock came, and Joey was obliged to return to put her babies to bed, the main topic of conversation was, "Where is Gwensi?"

CHAPTER 7

Gwensi Meets Some New Friends

It has to be recorded, however reluctantly, that, on this occasion, Gwensi won the game. Not until eight o'clock when the dusk was falling did she deign to leave her hiding-place and slip into the house. There she hid in a convenient cupboard near the kitchen door, watched her opportunity to raid the larder, and crept from there up the back-stairs, laden with half a pigeon-pie, a hunk of bread, a lump of margarine, and a wedge of cake, to her own little abode, where she devoured these dainties with good appetite, washed them down with a long drink of water, and then went to bed. There she was found at nine o'clock by the tearful Megan, fast asleep, and looking like a cherub.

Miss Annersley wisely left her to finish her slumbers, judging that in the first place she would be tired; and, in the second, nothing would please the young lady better than to know what consternation her goings-on had produced in the household. But at eight o'clock the next morning, she herself descended on the culprit to call her, and, having roused her, informed her that she was to get up and dress at once, and accompany her headmistress to the library.

What was more, the latter lady remained on guard all the time the small girl was dressing, and finally escorted her to the place of judgment, where she was informed that, since she obviously could not be trusted, she would not be left alone for a moment either that day or the next. Hence, for the whole of two days Gwensi went about in charge of someone or other, and hated it.

Jo was unable to get up to Plas Howell either day, as the triplets began fretting with new teeth, so she had her hands full. Mrs Russell put in an appearance on the second day, and spoke gently to the small rebel, trying to win the child's confidence. But Gwensi was filled with suspicious anger and remained sulkily silent. Madge finally let her go, and went off to discuss business with Miss Annersley, for the remainder of the staff were to arrive that evening, and the school would come on the morrow, so there was plenty to settle even yet.

Gwensi, left to herself, dawdled out of the room, and upstairs to her own sanctum, where she dropped down on the window seat and began to cry drearily. She had given her promise that she would not run away and hide again for another week—Madge had contrived to get so much out of her—so she was alone. She was still sobbing, when she heard the tap-tap of light feet, and then the door opened, and someone came in.

"What is the matter?" The voice was low-pitched, and very sweet, with an indefinable something in it that was not altogether English. Welsh Gwensi was too susceptible to music in any shape or form not to be attracted by it, and she scrubbed her eyes with her handkerchief, and looked up into one of the loveliest faces she had ever seen.

"Who are you?" she choked.

"I'm Robin—Robin Humphries. Joey told me she'd told you I was going to live at Plas Gwyn with her and the babies and Daisy. I was sorry not to be able to come up two days ago, but Daisy started toothache, so I stayed with her, explained the Robin, sitting down on the broad window seat, and laying an arm chummily round the thin shoulders that were still heaving. "You're Gwensi Howell, I know. Why are you crying, then, Gwensi? Can I help at all?"

Gwensi swallowed a sob before she replied with a sniff, "No—no one can. It's this *hateful* war! Ernest has gone and left me—and I do so lo-ove him! And I've no one left at all now."

"But he has not gone for always." Robin produced her own fresh handkerchief and tucked it into a hot hand as she spoke. "He will have leave—perhaps soon. Then he will come to you."

Gwensi rubbed her eyes with the handkerchief, finding its fresh coolness grateful to her poor, swollen eyes. "It may not be for ever so long, though," she said mournfully. "And—my home isn't *my* home any longer, for this horrid school has come to it."

Robin's beautiful face grew very serious. "But why should you call it horrid? You don't know anything about it yet. I've lived in it for ten years, and I have never found it so."

"Ten years?" A gleam of interest came into the dark eyes.

"Yes. My mother died when I was only six, and my father had to go on business to Russia, and could not take me. He had known Mrs Russell and her twin brother, Mr Bettany, when they were at school, and he heard all about the Chalet School, and left me with her. Later, when the Doctor married her, and they went to live at the Sonnalpe and have a Sanatorium for poor people who were ill with the same illness that took Mamma from us, Papa went as his secretary. That was in the Tyrol—Ah, my dear Tyrol!—and we were there till Hitler marched into Austria. Then the school had to leave, for they would not allow it to remain open. Joey—Mrs Maynard—and one or two others of us had to fly, for we had angered the Gestapo. Then we went to Guernsey, and began there. Now we have to leave again, in case the Germans should get there, and your brother has so kindly offered us his beautiful home while the war lasts. It was a great kindness, Gwensi. Will you spoil it for us by being miserable? It is still your home, and you are still living in it. If we were not here, then someone else would be, for this is a safety-zone. Perhaps they would have put Government offices here, and then you must have left. As it is, the school will use so much that they cannot say that any room is being wasted, and so you can remain. Isn't it better?"

Gwensi looked down. She was by no means ready to acknowledge that things *might* have been worse; but Robin's friendly voice certainly went a long way towards helping her to this belief.

"I—I've lived here so long," she whispered.

Robin pushed back the untidy hair from the hot face. "I

60

know. But so had we lived so long in the Tyrol. And we had to leave. You must ask Joey some day to tell you the story of how we fled—if she does not first put it into a book," she added laughingly.

"A book? Does—does Mrs Maynard *write books?*" Gwensi's voice was suitably awestruck.

"Why, of course she does. You may even have read some. She has had four published, and I know she has begun a new one, though she has not had any time to go on with it this past six weeks. But she began after Christmas, and five chapters are done, for I've read them."

"What are the names of her books?"

For answer, Robin glanced across at the bookcase and laughed again. "You have all four over there—even the new one that was published in November—just a fortnight after the triplets arrived."

Gwensi turned her head, and followed Robin's gaze. The next moment she had bounded from her seat, all her woes forgotten, and was tugging at *Tessa in the Tyrol.* "Do you mean she's Josephine M. Bettany? Oh, you *can't!* Why, she's my favourite writer! I loved this one—and all of them. Is it really her who's living at Plas Gwyn—the mother of those lovely babies? You don't really mean *that?*"

Again Robin's silvery laughter rang out. "But of course I do! Bring me *Cecily Holds the Fort.* See there!" And she opened the book and pointed to the dedication. "To my darling sister, Madge." That's Mrs Russell. Now give me *Patrol-Leader Nancy.* There! That's me!"

Gwensi bent over the book, her eyes devouring the dedication, "To my Robin."

"This is really you? Oh, how wonderful! What does it feel like to have a real book dedicated to you?"

"I am very proud," said Robin simply.

Gwensi looked at the book again. Then she pulled out the others and turned to the dedications which before now had not interested her. "Who are these, please? Anyone at the school?"

"*Tessa* is dedicated to her three great friends. Frieda is

here with us at Plas Gwyn. You will see her tomorrow, I expect. And Marie is with Mrs Russell, and her babies, and her sister Wanda and *her* babies too. As for Simone, she is Miss Lecoutier who is the maths mistress. They formed a quartet at school," explained Robin. "And *Gypsy Jocelyn* is dedicated to Dr Jack—Dr Maynard, that is, Joey's husband. She says that this new one she is writing must be for the babies, though it will be years before they will want to read it, of course."

"What is it called? Could you tell me?"

Robin considered. "I don't see why not. You won't talk about it, will you? Book titles are so often one thing when the book begins, and another when it is finished. It's called *Nancy Meets a Nazi*, and it's a kind of sequel to *Patrol-Leader Nancy*."

"It sounds *thrilling*!" breathed Gwensi.

"Oh, it is! Joey writes from experience, you see. Now won't you come down and meet Daisy and her chum, Beth Chester? Joey told Daisy all about you the other day, and she's dying to meet you because you're almost like a twin as your birthdays are exactly the same. Do come!"

Gwensi rose. "Yes, I'd like to. Do you know," she added confidentially, "I've never known another girl who was *exactly* my own age. What is Daisy like, please?"

Robin looked at her consideringly. "She's not a bit like you. She's so fair—primrose fair, Joey says. Her hair really is yellow, and she has blue eyes and pink-and-white cheeks. She's very pretty—as pretty as you are. Only you are so dark, and she is, as our Head Girl, Cornelia Flower, would say, "an honest-to-goodness blonde." And Beth Chester, who is her chum, has chestnut curls and violet eyes. You'll fit in very well, I think. Sponge your face, Gwensi, and then come along. There's heaps to do, and very little time to do it."

Mesmerised by this lovely girl's sweet voice and equally sweet manner, Gwensi did as she was told, and presently was following Robin down the great staircase, face and hands washed, black hair neatly tied back and looking generally better. At the foot of the stairs two or three girls were standing; one was plainly older than herself, the others of her own age; and from Robin's description, she recognised Daisy Venables and Beth Chester.

"Girls," said Robin, a hand on the small shoulder which was not so much below her own, "this is Gwensi Howell. Corney, here's the first of our new girls this term. And these are Daisy and Beth, Gwensi."

Cornelia Flower turned a kindly smile on the little girl, and said a few pleasant words in her markedly American voice. Then she and Robin went off, and the three thirteen-year-olds were left to make friends.

Gwensi felt suddenly shy; but Daisy did not know the meaning of the word, and slipped a hand chummily into her arm. "Rob says you've lived here for ages, Gwensi. You can show us everything, can't you? Come along and do it, there's a dear. We're dying to know the place, aren't we, Beth?"

"Rather!" responded Beth. "Can you show us where our form gardens are likely to be, Gwensi? I'm aching to know. I'm going to take up gardening as a profession, you know. Daddy says if I do well at school he'll try and send me to Swanley—that's a college for gardeners."

"I—I think they're behind the shrubbery," stammered Gwensi. "Will you come, and I'll show you."

She led the way out of the house, and round to the side, where the great shubbery made a real plantation. Behind this lay a broad, sunny patch which had been a meadow; but under Miss Annersley's instructions it had been dug up; and now six long, wide beds were ready, all waiting for the young gardeners. Iron notices driven into the earth at the foot of each told to which form each belonged, and Daisy and Beth pounced with cries of joy on the one marked "Form III."

"This is ours! Oh, good! It'll get heaps of sun; and yet there's quite a good deal of shade from those chestnuts," said Beth professionally. "We ought to be able to do well with it."

"What do you suppose we'll grow?" asked Daisy.

"I don't know. I don't know what the soil here is good for. Perhaps Gwensi can tell us, can you, Gwensi?"

"I don't quite know what you mean," said Gwensi.

"Well, what sort of vegetables do well in this part of the world?"

Gwensi shook her head. "We grow potatoes, and cabbages—and parsnips—and the usual things," she said, racking her brains for anything outstanding. "And we always have lots of lettuces and so on. Oh, and I know!" —joyfully, as a sudden recollection came to her—"asparagus does awfully well here. We have an enormous bed in the kitchen garden."

"Asparagus? It's rather—well, a bit of a luxury," returned Beth. "I wonder if they'll let us grow it? Are the roots awfully dear, d'you know, Gwensi?"

"I don't think they call them roots. I'm almost sure they grow from crowns. I've heard Evan Evans say so. And if you want any, I'll ask for them, and he'll give them to us, of course."

"Will he?" Beth sounded dubious. "Well, you can ask him, anyhow. He can only say no, I suppose."

"He's in the kitchen garden now. I saw him go past my window with a wheelbarrow an hour ago. Let's go and ask him now," proposed Gwensi.

No sooner said than done. The trio raced off to the kitchen garden where Evan Evans, a short, sturdy Welshman in his fifties, was busy setting potatoes. At sight of "Miss Gwensi fach" his face broke into a smile, and he uttered a few words which sounded like so much gibberish to the two aliens. Gwensi answered him swiftly in the same tongue, and the smile broadened. He shook his head but she insisted and, after ten minutes' argument, he evidently gave way for he nodded, but uttering a sentence or two in a warning voice, at which Gwensi danced a jig of glee.

"What are you saying? What is it all about?" cried Daisy. "Can't he speak English, Gwensi? What did you say to him?"

"Yes, I speak English," said Evan Evans himself, speaking it with a broad Welsh accent.

"But it's easier in Welsh, of course," explained Gwensi. "He says the ground will need a great deal of preparation; but if our gardening mistress will agree, he will show us what to do. We can't expect much or *anything* this year. But next year, if all goes well, we might have something to show for it. Oh, and Beth, he says you will make anything grow. He says you have *green* fingers. That means that you're a born gardener."

Beth blushed purple at this. "How awfully nice of him. I—I *am* keen on it," she stammered. "What else could we grow there?"

"Beans and peas," said Evan Evans. "And broccoli, and carrots, and onions. They will all do well if sown now."

"What about artichokes?" demanded Daisy.

He shook his head. "The ground would not be ready. It must be done in early autumn, and well manured. But other vegetables—yes."

"What must you do that we can't do it now?" demanded Gwensi, speaking in English for the sake of her new friends.

"Why, look you, it must be dug deep—two spits down—that is, the deepness twice over of a spade. Then you must add manure, and wood ash. And then, sprinkle it with salt, which will help to keep the weeds away. And you must leave the earth open all winter, that the rain and the snow may work all together, and it is dug with a fork in March. *Then*, when April comes, you will put in your young plants."

"And what happens then?" asked Daisy, who had been listening to all this with wide-eyed interest. "Weeding and watering, I suppose?"

"Yes, indeed. And here, we do not allow the plants to flower the first year, so as to get very good, fine plants with a strong growth," explained Evan, becoming more and more Welshy in his earnestness. "So you will have very good, fine tubers the second year."

"The *second* year!" repeated Daisy in dismay. "Oh dear! Is it another vegetable that needs years and years before you can eat it?"

Again the slow smile broadened as he replied, "It is better so!" What more he might have said they were not to know then, for at that moment Miss Annersley appeared to call them to their tea, and they had to leave him. Beth was at school now, as was Cornelia. But Daisy and Robin, once tea was over, had to get their bicycles and say goodbye, for they had a good two-and-a-half miles to go home. The three boarders saw them off, and then strolled down to the school garden-beds to discuss the important question of garden crops; for the Chalet School had taken as its war-time motto "Dig for Victory," and the Head Girl was determined that every girl should work, as far as in her lay, to that end.

When eight o'clock summoned the two thirteen-year-olds to bed, it found Gwensi almost reconciled to her new life, so full of interest was she, and so marvellous did it seem to her that even she could help the war on, if it were only by doing her share of weeding faithfully.

CHAPTER 8

The School Returns

The next day, the school proper made its appearance. The staff had all come the previous day, but the girls had seen little of them till breakfast of the opening day. Then Gwensi was presented to Miss Wilson, who taught science and geography; Mademoiselle Lachenais, who was responsible for modern languages and Latin; Miss Lecoutier—the "Simone" of the dedication in *Tessa in the Tyrol*—who taught mathematics; Miss Phipps, who would take charge of the Kindergarten, and her assistant, a very charming girl of twenty-two, whom the "old" girls saluted as "Gillian" before they hurriedly changed it for "Miss Linton"; and Miss Cochrane, who directed the major portion of the school's music. Robin explained later that really gifted people were the pupils of the old Austrian master, Herr Anserl. Besides these, there were Mr Denny, a long-haired individual, who sported an Elizabethan beard as well as Elizabethan ideals, and who took singing throughout the school; and his sister, Miss Denny, who "helped out", to quote herself.

"But who is coming to us for history, I wonder?" said Robin anxiously when the girls were left alone for their elevenses. "Last term, we had Miss Stewart, but now she is married, and I've heard nothing about her successor as yet. Corney, do you know?"

Cornelia shook her head. "Not a murmur. Polly—" she turned to Polly Heriot, another Senior, "— have *you* heard nothing?"

But, like the Head Girl, Polly was blankly ignorant, so they had to wait till the mistress in question turned up. Then the girls began to arrive and Gwensi, shy and, once more, rather inclined to resent this incursion of her home, drew back into a corner and watched the big buses chartered for the occasion as they drew up before the circular steps and discharged their burdens.

She saw Robin fling herself on a pigtailed individual of her own age with a cry of "Lorenz! But I thought you weren't returning!"

Lorenz laughed as she warmly returned her friend's embraces. "So did I. But Papa has left Hungary and is come to England to live. So I shall be here. And there"— she turned to a shy-looking child of about nine, who was sufficiently like her for people to know they were sisters— "is Ilonka, my baby sister, who is joining us this term. Lonka, this is Robin of whom I have told you."

Gwensi's eyes left the little group then, for Daisy had uttered a wild shriek of joy and was welcoming three girls vociferously. "Here you are! Isn't this gorgeous? How d'you like it? Have you had decent hols? Gillian Linton has come back as a Kindergarten mistress!" She poured forth her questions and information breathlessly.

"What a magnificent place!" exclaimed one of the girls, a dark-haired, vivacious-looking person of thirteen. "It's a regular *mansion*! I say! They *have* done us proud this time!"

"Who's here?" questioned one of the others. "Are we getting any new girls this term? Tell us all the news, Daisy."

"How are Joey and the triplets?" queried a quiet-looking Senior whom Cornelia had addressed as "Vi, old girl!" before reddening, and adding "Jolly glad to see you back again. And here's Jeanne as well. How are things in France, Jeanne?"

Jeanne shook her head doubtfully. "I cannot say, Corney. Shall we go and report? Then you can show us our dormies. The children will be exclaiming for ages yet."

Gwensi felt rather neglected. But not for long. Daisy had been well trained, and before she had left Plas Gwyn that morning, Jo had called her aside, and reminded her to look after her new friend.

"Remember, Daisy, it's all very new to her—and rather hard lines, too, in some ways. Look after her, and see that she isn't left out of anything, won't you?"

Daisy had promised; so as soon as the first raptures were over, she looked round for Gwensi, and promptly spied her, and dragged her out of her corner. "Come along, Gwensi! Girls, this is Gwensi Howell whose brother has been decent enough to let us have his house for the duration. Gwensi, these are Mélanie Kerdec, who comes from Brittany; Nicole de Saumarez from Jersey; and Isabel Allan—*she's* from Selkirk in Scotland. Where's Bethy? We want her to come and show us their dormy.''

Beth Chester appeared at that moment with a brown-eyed, brown-haired thirteen-year-old in tow, whom she introduced as Nancy Canton; and presently the six were running up the backstairs to seek the dormitory which the five were to share. Beth, her small sister—another Nancy— and the five-year-old twin brothers who were in the Kindergarten, were all to be boarders, as their mother was living just out of Armiford, and it was too far for the youngsters to travel daily.

At the top of the stairs they fell into the clutches of Matron, who welcomed them calmly, told them where they were to go, and bade them first deposit their cases and make themselves tidy, and then go to the library to report to the Head.

All told, it was the most exciting time Gwensi had ever had; and when tea-time came, and she sat down in her appointed place between Daisy and a saintly-looking character of her own age whose name was Jacqueline le Pelley, she had not had a moment to feel miserable or sulky or lonely. She eyed the crowds of girls sitting on either side of the long trestle-tables, with their pretty checked cloths and bowls of gay spring flowers, and decided that things weren't going to be quite as bad as she had feared.

After tea the newcomers had to unpack and be ready for General Assembly, which would take place in Hall at half-past six. Gwensi, having nothing to do, was much in request among Daisy's crowd to help, and got her first taste of community life in a very jolly form.

She was down in the hall, helping Daisy and Beth to sort

out suitcases, when a big car drove up before the wide steps, and a tall man with a keen, clever face got out, followed by three girls. Daisy glanced up and then nudged the other two. "New girls! What a crowd there are this term! And so many in the Senior School! It's rather fun, isn't it?"

"We were over fifty last term," responded Beth in an undertone. "Any idea how many we shall be this, Daisy?"

"Not the slightest—though I did hear Jo say to Auntie Madge that she wouldn't be surprised if we reached one hundred in September. There was something about a school somewhere near here that had stopped, and a lot of the girls coming here instead. P'raps it's them," said Daisy with a great lack of grammar. "I *have* noticed that two or three of them seem to stick together. Gwensi, do you know what school it was?"

Gwensi shook her head. "I don't. Megan might know. She gets all the hanes—"

"All the *what*?" interrupted Beth, pausing with Biddy O'Ryan's suitcase in one hand, and Isabel Allan's bundle of rugs in the other.

"It's Welsh for gossip," explained Gwensi.

Daisy heaved a portentous sigh. "I never knew such a school as this for languages! In the Tyrol we all had to talk English, French, and German. Then we have one or two Italians; and Lorenz Maico is Hungarian; and Sigrid Björnesson—she's that big, very fair girl who went off with Robin—she's Norwegian. Now you're Welsh. It's a real Tower of Babel!"

"But we haven't got to learn to talk in all them, *have* we?" gasped Gwensi, horror-stricken.

"French and English we *must*, of course. And so far we've kept up our German. I don't know if we shall go on with it, though."

By this time, the gentleman had entered the hall, with the three girls beside him, so the three Middles ceased talking, and went on with their work in silence. Mary, one of the parlour-maids, came to lead them away to the library where Miss Annersley, having duly welcomed all her pupils, had been sitting enjoying a quiet cup of tea with Miss Wilson, and discussing various points that came up.

"How many are we?" demanded Bill, as she helped herself to a cress sandwich.

"Eighty-seven so far. Of course, we should never have got so many new girls this term if it hadn't been for that Medbury school closing. As it is, we've got ten of theirs. I understand that Miss Cundell never took more than twenty-five at most, and when the school closed she had only nineteen. She told me that she had given the parents two terms' notice, so one or two were sent to boarding-school at once. Three of the elder girls have gone to the grammer school at Weonister, which is seven miles from Medbury; the rest are, for the most part, either to go to other boarding-schools or have changed to a small day-school which had been begun in the same place. But they are all Juniors."

"And then there are the two Wallace girls from the Vicarage," added Bill musingly. "And that doctor's girl from St Wynedd's—what is her name?"

"You mean Terry Prosser," laughed the Head. "I shall never forget her face when I saluted her as 'Theresa'. Well, 'Terry' is certainly not nearly so stiff, and I have no real objection to it."

"You couldn't! Otherwise, Robin would have to be 'Cecilia', and Polly 'Hildegard'," interjected Bill with a chuckle. "Can't you see their faces?"

"I can," Miss Annersley was beginning, when a tap at the door announced the arrival of Mary and the four visitors.

"Dr Marilliar," said Mary; and when the smallest of the trio of girls had entered, she shut the door and came away, to be caught at the end of the passage by three eager Middles.

"Mary! That's the big doctor from Medbury. He knows my brother. Are they coming here to school?" demanded Gwensi excitedly.

"H'ssh, Miss Gwensi! Madam'll hear you, and you didn't ought to be here," said Mary.

"She can't if you shut the door properly. Do tell, Mary cariad!" implored Gwensi.

"I don't know anything to tell, Miss Gwensi. But I believe there's luggage in the car and on the back. Now let me go, or Megan'll be that cross with me." And Mary wrenched herself free from the young lady's grasp and escaped kitchenwards.

Left alone, the Middles looked at each other. "Three more, and I thought everyone had come!" said Daisy. "I say! At this rate the school *will* be catching up again. D'you know, Gwensi, the term before we left the Tyrol we had over two hundred and fifty. Supposing we get up to that again! Wouldn't it be gorgeous!"

At this point Cornelia Flower appeared to ask if they had not finished their work yet, as Matron wanted the cases brought upstairs. "And it's just on half-past five, and you've got to make yourselves fit to be seen. I guess you'd better make tracks, and make 'em pretty fast at that," wound up the Head Girl.

Thus called to order, the three fled, and when Miss Annersley came along ten minutes later to escort the big doctor to the door while Miss Wilson took the three girls upstairs, the hall was empty.

A little later, at five to six, to be accurate, a bell rang, and the school left its dormitories, and began to go quietly down the backstairs to Hall, as the big drawing-room was hereafter to be known. Only the five prefects descended by the great flight, as was their privilege. Daisy and Beth had explained all this to Gwensi who, at the time, had resented the new restriction. However, in the excitement of the first night of term, she forgot her resentment, and went with as good grace as the rest, duly escorted by her first two friends, who squeezed her between them on to the green-painted form which stood in the row marked "Form III". The prefects were accommodated with forms at one side of the dais, and the rest of the Sixth, six in number, were at the other side. The Kindergarten babies sat on cushions in the front row, and behind them came the rows of forms, rising from First to Fifth. The staff filed in, and took their seats on a row of chairs placed at the back of the dais, and when a pleasant-faced girl of about twenty-three or four, wearing glasses and a broad smile, accompanied them, there came a gasp from various points in the room which told Gwensi that something exciting had happened. However, the Head followed hard on the heels of the staff, so no one could say anything, and the little Welsh girl had to subside, and await events.

Miss Annersley bade everyone welcome, and told them briefly how it was that the school was housed in Plas Howell. There were no examination results to announce; but, as she said, there were a good many items of news personal to the school.

"First of all," she said, "we must give another of our old girls a welcome as a member of staff. You elder girls will remember Mary Burnett when she was our Head Girl. Now she has come back to us to take the place of Miss Stewart, our history mistress. And I must thank Peggy and Kitty Burnett for managing to keep their sister's secret so well."

There was a round of applause at this. Those who remembered Mary Burnett at school knew her to have been a great favourite and an excellent Head Girl. The rest joined in from force of example.

Miss Annersley gave them their heads for a minute. Then she held up her hand for silence. "Save a little of your ardour," she told them laughingly. "I have a good deal more news for you. Juliet Carrick, who was not only at school as a pupil, but also was Head of the Annexe for two or three years, and was married shortly before we left the Tyrol, has written to Madame, as we still love to call Mrs Russell, and announced the arrival of her son three weeks ago. Juliet is evacuating to this part of the world next month, so we may hope to see her and the baby before very long. Next, I have to announce that Joey has had a letter from Hilary Burn, who tells us that she is finishing her course of physical training at the end of this term, and

73

hopes to join us as games mistress in September. I will say nothing about Gillian Linton joining us as a Kindergarten mistress, for most of you knew of it last term. Joyce has sent word that she is engaged to be married—she is at present visiting her fiancé's people—but she is coming here afterwards to share Gillian's rooms in the village until her wedding, which is to take place in June so that the school may be present at it. Ilonka Barkocz is at the School of Economics in London, taking a course there, and when she has finished, she tells me that she hopes to get a post as lecturer at one of the smaller English universities. As you all heard last term, Monsieur Barkocz died at Christmas, so Madame Barkocz is coming to England with Irma, who will go to the Royal College of Music with Renée Lecoutier. Elsie Carr, Anne Seymour, Nancy Wilmot, Ida Reaveley, and Irene Silksworth are all in the Wrens, and working well. Margia Stevens, who had started on a concert tour of Australia just before war broke out, is now in South Africa, where she has another tour to complete before she returns home. The list of V.A.D.s among our old girls is so lengthy that I won't stop to read it, but will pin it up on the noticeboard so that you may read it for yourselves. Finally, from New Zealand and India comes news of two old members of the staff. Miss Maynard, now Mrs Bennett, has a second daughter; and Miss Leslie, whom most of you will remember, and who is now Mrs Stephenson, has twin sons. I think you all know that Miss Stewart is on her way to Singapore with her husband. Oh yes; one more item of news. Herr Laubach, who was our art master in the Tyrol, has finally succeeded in escaping, and will join us here in a fortnight's time in his old capacity. Frau Laubach died six months ago, as I think some of you know; but he has just succeeded in getting away now.''

Once more she paused, and once more the school took advantage of it to applaud loudly. Finally she spoke again.

"One last thing I have to say to you, girls. You have not, I hope, forgotten our Peace League? As things are, we can do very little for those of its members who are still in enemy

74

country. But remember, they are Chalet School girls, who have been trained in the same ideals as you have. God alone knows what these girls may be suffering now, and there is only one thing we can do to help them. Let us all do it with all our might. We mean to gain the victory; for, make no mistake, this evil thing called Nazism that has reared its head above the world like a venomous snake must perish as all evil must. There are many in Germany, more in Austria, who hate it as we do. Theirs may be a martyrdom which, in God's great mercy, *we* may be spared. I hope we are. But those who belong to our League are part of us, even though we cannot communicate with them at present. Those of you who were with us last Christmas term know that Dr von Ahlen, Frieda Mensch's husband, and Herr von Gluck, the husband of Wanda von Eschenau, are free from a concentration camp and its horrors, thanks to the courage of one of our girls who signed the vow of the Peace League. We do not know what may have become of that girl. We do not know if her work has been discovered and she has had to pay dearly for it. We do not even know her name. But time will tell us this and all other stories. Meanwhile, let us do the one thing we *can* do. Let us pray for our League and all its members, that God will keep them safe and that some time we may meet—if not in this world, then in the next. And let us all live up to the splendid ideals set forth in our vow, so that when peace comes—as come it must in God's own time—we shall be ready to turn it to the finest and noblest use we can. Joey Bettany—Joey Maynard now—has written a prayer for us to use, and before we break up now, I will ask you to repeat it after me, phrase by phrase. Later, you will all be given a chance to learn it, so that you may use it every day. And remember: this is the least we owe to those German and Austrian members who are 'carrying on' amid such terrible doings as we read of, and we must pay our debt faithfully. Let us pray.''

The girls knelt down, so did the staff; and they repeated after the Head the words of the brief prayer Joey had written for the League: ''O God, our Heavenly Father, watch over all members of the Chalet School Peace League, we beseech Thee. Keep us all safe in Thy Fatherly care. Help us to live up to the ideals we have set before us. When peace shall come, help us to be ready to use it nobly and faithfully. And grant that in Thine own time we shall all meet again. For Christ's sake, Amen.''

CHAPTER 9

Gardens and Gardening

"You mean that we really take gardening as a school subject?"

"Of course. Why shouldn't we?" Kitty Burnett raised her eyebrows at Jocelyn Redford's amazed face. "Madame says that more and more girls will be taking up gardening as a profession, and it's necessary to learn early—now more than ever."

"Well, I think it's simply marvellous!" Clare Danvers, another of the new girls from Medbury, put her word in. "I hadn't thought of it as a profession—as a matter of fact I thought I'd better do secretarial work, as it seemed to be the only thing I could be any good at. But I always have loved messing about in the garden from the time I was a tiny kid and used to pick up the weeds after Dad and put them in my wheelbarrow and trundle them to the rubbish heap for vegetable manure. To learn it really properly and with a professional expert seems too good to be true."

The Fifth Form were all out, viewing the great beds which had been prepared for the school gardens, and Kitty Burnett, Amy Stevens, Enid Sothern, and Suzanne Mercier had been explaining to the newcomers exactly what was expected of them. The Fifth consisted of six of the original form from Sarres in Guernsey, and five new girls, all of whom had come from Braemar House at Medbury. Robin, Jeanne de Marné, and Lorenz Maïco had been moved up to the Sixth this term, and Robin and Lorenz had been prefects at Easter in any case. Amy Stevens should have gone with them, since she was a year older than any of them; but continued attacks of cold had kept her back in her work so she had to stay behind, much to their disgust.

Of the new girls, Jocelyn Redford had already told of her intention to become a gym mistress, and Monica Marilliar, the great doctor's only daughter, had voiced the same intention. Pretty Myfanwy Tudor, second daughter of the Rector of Medbury, was working at music, and would be a pupil of gruff old Herr Anserl; but so far neither Clare Danvers nor Ernestine Benedict, the two remaining members of the form, had said what they wished to do. Now Clare was gazing delightedly at the stretch of bare, reddish-brown earth before her, and making plans for her future. The rest of the form turned to Ernestine hopefully.

"What do you intend to do, Ernestine?" asked Amy. "I'm going to teach, of course. I've always meant to. And Kitty wants to be a nurse, and so does Greta."

"That's what I want," replied Ernestine in the soft voice that they had all noted already. "I'm as strong as a horse, and I love looking after sick people. I don't mind what I do to help them. So I'm going to nurse—I hope."

"And what about the rest of you?" demanded Monica briskly. "What do *you* mean to do, Enid?"

Enid Sothern, an impish-looking young person of fifteen, smiled. "I'd never meant to do anything but stay at home and help Mums. I've no need to work, and Dad says it's absolutely wicked for girls who have plenty to take the work from girls who haven't. With this wretched war on I want to be a V.A.D. as soon as I'm old enough. But that's got to wait a year or two, unfortunately. In the meantime, I'm knitting for all I'm worth. And, of course, I'm going to pitch in at the garden. However, Dorothy is the most ambitious of the lot of us. She wants to be a surgeon, if you please."

Once more the form turned this time to look at boyish-looking Dorothy Brentham, who reddened under their gaze. "Well, I've always wanted it," she said sturdily. "Daddy's a doctor, so I expect I inherit it. Anyhow, I'm going to have a stab at it."

"Yes, do! And Kitty and Greta and I will nurse your cases for you! We might run a nursing-home," suggested Ernestine eagerly.

"We might *not*," retorted Dorothy. "You folk will be

fully-fledged nurses before I get through with my qualifications. But Daddy says that he'll back me right through, seeing I'm a one-and-only, and not a boy as he'd hoped. So that's all right. I'm taking School Certificate this term, and if I get a good enough grade then I'll drop some subjects—history, and literature, and stuff like that—and go all out for science and biology, and try to get Higher for both.''

"I'm doing School Cert. too—worse luck!'' laughed Monica. "How many of us will there be? Anyone know?''

"A good many, I think,'' said Kitty. "Not Amy, of course; nor you, didn't you say, Myfanwy? But all the rest of us, and most of the Sixth. You see, we really only started school again last September; and in the Tyrol we didn't take it.''

"Here's Miss Everett,'' said Greta, a shy, soft-voiced Highlander, who generally had very little to say.

The Fifth ceased their discussion and came to attention as Miss Everett, the gardening mistress, came briskly down the path to them.

Unlike the majority of the staff, she was visiting, since her home was with the Lucys, who were living three miles away. She was a tall, very sturdy person, neat in her stout, corduroy breeches and leather leggings, her short brown hair tucked into a brown beret. The Fifth had met her once before, when the weather had been too bad for them to do any work on their garden, and on that occasion she had given them a talk on soils which the new girls had somehow connected with geography. But this was a perfect day, with bright sunshine, a fresh breeze, and just a few fleecy white clouds drifting across the sky. School had started just one week previously, and they all felt settled in, and quite ready for anything. Miss Everett marched up to them, and saluted them with a "Good morning, girls!'' as breezy as the day itself.

"This your bed?'' she continued, giving it a swift glance. "Good plot—well in the sun, but liable to catch some shade in the middle of the day from the trees at that end. Well, let's see what's been done.''

79

"Evan Evans the gardener says he's dug it down two spits, Miss Everett," said Kitty, who, as form prefect, took the lead. "He dug in a little manure, but not much, he says, because it's lain fallow so long that it shouldn't need much."

"Quite right. What did he do with the sods?"

"Dug them under, to make natural manure," replied Enid Sothern.

"Quite right again. Now, girls, what do you propose to grow in your bed? Give me your ideas, and then we shall begin to know where we are."

A barrow stood near, and Miss Everett sat down on one of the handles, cocking one leg over the other. The form stood round her, eager to give her all their ideas at once, so she waved them into silence.

"One at a time, please! Amy Stevens, what have you to say?"

"Potatoes, Miss Everett. We can't have too many with such a crowd of us, can we? And it's such a useful vegetable."

"Quite right, Amy; but it's getting rather late on for many potatoes—second week in May. Still, we might put in a few rows of the late-sowing varieties." She got up, and went over to kneel by the bed, and examine the soil. "This is good soil—not too heavy, and rich without being too rich—which encourages disease."

"How should we plant them, Miss Everett?" asked Clare.

"We'll make what are called drills, Clare. You girls must rake the soil thoroughly till it is as fine as possible. Then we'll draw lines with the hoes—in this case, three feet apart. If we were planting earlies two feet would be enough."

"Do we just draw our hoes along the ground—not dig at all? That seems easy," said Monica, who was standing next to Clare.

Miss Everett laughed, showing a row of white, even teeth which gleamed in her brown face. "Lazy, Monica? Oh, dear no! Potato drills ought to be about four inches deep.

Still, that won't give you much trouble as the earth has been so thoroughly dug and loosened."

"But how do we keep the drills straight?" demanded Enid. "I'm sure *I* couldn't. Drawing never *was* a gift of mine."

"We'll put down a peg here." Miss Everett indicated the spot with her foot. "Then we'll put down a peg at the opposite side—you can measure from the corners if you like to be really accurate—and join them with fine twine. That will be ruler enough for you to trace your drills. Then you'll dig down four inches, and when that's done, you'll set your potatoes. How many are there of you? Eleven? What an awkward number! Never mind, I'll make the sixth pair. Two to each drill, and that will give you six rows. Come along and get your pegs and string."

She dealt them out a peg each, and set Clare and Kitty to measuring for the top drill. The lines were taken from this, and presently the six rows of fine white twine were stretched across the broad bed. Then came the hoeing, and the girls drew their lines meticulously, one of the partners doing the drawing, while the other came behind with a light spade and deepened it to approximately four inches. Naturally, the hoers were finished before the diggers, so when they had set their implements to one side, they were bidden to get spades and dig also.

At length it was done, and then the mistress directed their attention to several big baskets full of seed potatoes. "There are your potatoes, girls. Anyone know what to do next?"

"Put them in and cover them over?" ventured Amy.

Miss Everett shook her head. "Each of you take one. Now look. Do you see the "eyes"? Those are really buds. To get a good crop of sound, good-sized potatoes you must remove all except one—or, at most, two. Choose the finest-looking, and cut out the others. There are your knives. Go ahead."

Laughing at this, the girls set to work, and soon all had brown hands from the potato juice. Before long, one or two people were complaining that they ached between forefinger and thumb with the necessity of holding them in the cramped position necessary for cutting. However, Miss Everett would allow no slacking, and it was not until what she considered a large enough supply had been prepared that she allowed them a rest. Then she gave each couple a basket, and showed them how to "set" the potato, with the remaining shoot or shoots uppermost.

"Not too near, girls," she warned them. "Fifteen inches apart; remember the fruit wants room to spread. By the way, who can tell me what part of the plant potatoes are?"

Silence! Botany was not a subject that had been much taught at the Chalet School, where they had gone in for chemistry and physics. With a smile, she took pity on them. "It's a stem—an underground stem," she told them.

"A *stem*!" The chorus was one of disbelief. The entire form were of the opinion that the mistress was trying to pull their legs. But she nodded emphatically, and repeated her statement.

"Really, girls, that is what it is. A greatly swollen stem, of course. But it is a stem for all that."

"Then—are carrots and turnips and parsnips stems, too, Miss Everett?" asked Clare, beginning to revise her ideas on plants with some rapidity.

"Oh dear, no," said Miss Everett. "The potato belongs to the same family as the nightshade. The turnip is one of the brassica family—the same as the cabbage; and the carrot is yet another."

The girls gasped. "And—and is the parsnip another again?" asked Kitty rather faintly.

"No, the parsnip and the carrot belong to the same order."

The bell rang for elevenses as Miss Everett finished speaking, and she nodded to them. "Leave the potatoes for the moment, and run along and get your cocoa and biscuits. Come straight back when the bell goes, though. I want those potatoes finished this morning."

They left their baskets and knives, and went off to wash

their hands before joining the throng in the big old kitchen where cocoa and biscuits were served from a long refectory table by Megan, assisted by two more of the maids. The Juniors had their break at another time, since their lessons ended half an hour earlier, so it was not quite such a crowd as it might have been.

"And a good thing, too," declared Greta, surveying her hands with dismay. "I've scrubbed and scrubbed, and I can't get this stain off."

"Try essence of lemon," advised Polly Heriot, who was passing at the time and heard her. "It'll remove most stains."

"You'll have to put up with it just now, anyhow," added Kitty cheerfully. "After all, Greta, it just shows that you're trying to do *something* to help with the war. Don't be a fuss!"

Thus advised, Greta took her cocoa and sipped it, while the chatter eddied round her. But, war or no war, she determined to try Polly's suggestion, being a fastidious young person.

After elevenses the Fifth wended their way back to their plot, and, with Miss Everett watching them carefully, began to set their potatoes with due care for distance to allow of cropping.

"Late potatoes are generally what are called 'heavy croppers'," she informed them.

"Anything like the lovely cropper I came just now over that rake?" murmured frivolous Jocelyn, who had just measured her full length on the earth over a rake that had been carelessly left lying at the side of the bed. "*That* was a heavy cropper all right."

Monica, who received this gem of wit, exploded, and Miss Everett looked up rather startled. Then, as her eyes were caught by the condition of Jocelyn's corduroys and jumper, she joined in the laugh. "No, not that sort of cropper at all, Jocelyn. When gardeners talk of 'heavy cropper' they simply mean that it gives a good crop."

"How much ought each plant to give, Miss Everett?" asked Amy.

"The average is about two and a half pounds. But, of course, some plants give less, and others will give more. It varies."

"Oh, how my back aches!" sighed Kitty Burnett half an hour later, as she straightened up for a moment. "Planting potatoes is no joke. I think it would be quite a good idea to set Hitler and his army at it for, say, a month on end. *That* would larn them!"

Miss Everett, who, as some of the girls complained, had a most unholy trick of always being where you did *not* want her, came up behind in time to overhear this remark. "English as she is spoke," she said sweetly. "Really, Kitty!"

Kitty flushed, but said nothing. After all, there was nothing she *could* say. But for the rest of the term, if she had a remark to make that she preferred the mistress not to hear, she looked round cautiously before she made it. Meanwhile she bent her back again, and, at long length, all those potatoes were in.

"Finished?" asked Miss Everett of Clare and Enid who had finished first. "Then get your rakes, and draw the earth lightly over so that you cover them. Rake it up, so that they are about five or six inches deep when you have finished."

"Do we water them next?" asked Enid innocently.

Miss Everett shouted with laughter at the idea. "My dear Enid! Farmers usually plant a field at a time. Who's going to water that, do you think? Potatoes aren't like flower seeds. No, I'm afraid you must leave them to nature after this—so far as watering is concerned, anyhow."

"Is there anything else to do?" asked Amy.

"Plenty. When the stems are about seven or eight inches high, you must earth them up to about one inch from the top. And, of course, you must weed. But it isn't hand-weeding," she added, taking pity on the long faces round her. "You'll hoe round the plants, being very careful not to chop any of the shoots off, of course. Later, in the trenches that will be formed by the earthing-up, we'll plant cabbages or some other form of greens. That is known as 'intercropping,' and is the most economical way of using your space."

The bell for the end of morning school rang just as the last pair finished their line, and Miss Everett dismissed a class that was hot, sticky, weary, and aching, but, for all that, glowing with the consciousness that it had done a little towards helping the nation; and also ready for dinner, and glad to settle down in the afternoon to a comparatively restful lesson in French translation, followed by an hour's needlework.

CHAPTER 10

The Prefects in Council

"I like the Fifth; the babes are little dears, taking them by and large, and the Thirds are quite a jolly little set. But, oh! how I yearn for a cane and the right to use it on the Fourth!" Thus Polly Heriot as she entered the prefects' room and slammed the door after her.

The rest of the prefects looked up from their various occupations.

"What have they been doing *now*?" asked Violet Allison.

"What haven't they? Breaking rules right and left; leaving gates open so that the cattle and sheep wander; upsetting the entire staff—"

"Who has been getting at *you*?" demanded Robin shrewdly.

"Bill!" Polly flung herself into a wicker chair which creaked loud protests at such treatment, and stared moodily out of the window. "She wanted to know why I—the prefect on duty—wasn't at the foot of the stairs before dinner to see that the girls went up quietly and in order? As I was engaged in tying up Bride Bettany's cut finger at the moment—Matey was busy with the Ozanne twins who were involved in the same accident, and both, so far as I can gather, likely to come out with black eyes of the finest grade, so she turned Bride over to me—I couldn't very well be there, and didn't see one of you folk to hand over to."

"Why didn't you tell Bill so?" demanded Lorenz.

"So I did when I got a chance. But she was foaming at the mouth, and didn't let me get a word in edgeways till she was through. She apologized, of course, when she understood; but by that time she'd said all she'd got to say—and she's got a tongue like a nutmeg-grater when she's aroused, as you very well know."

"What had the Ozannes and Bride Bettany been up to?"

asked Cornelia, not ceasing for one moment to knit.

"A bicycle race through the big hoops held by some of the others."

"*What*!" The exclamation came as a chorus from the other seven.

"Mad, wasn't it? But you know what those Ozanne twins are. They look as if butter wouldn't melt in their mouths, but they think of the most impossible things to do—and do them. So far as I can make out, Vanna suggested it, and Nella and Bride both leapt at the idea. They all have child's cycles, of course, so that part of the business was no trouble to them. They got some of their own tribe to hold those huge hoops they have for hoop drill across the course, and the idea was to ride through."

"Mussy me!" ejaculated Cornelia, who had never been behindhand in mad tricks in her own early days. "Were the little ninnies mad?"

"Oh, it would have been all right if they hadn't made a race of it," said Polly. "They can all ride well, and there's no trick about it. But, as far as I can gather, the three of them converged on one hoop, and all tried to get through at once. Bride managed to get through before she fell off. The twins barged into each other. Vanna's elbow caught Nella's right eye. Julie Lucy was holding the hoop, and she seems to have squalled and let it go, and fallen on top of the heap, and her foot, in some miraculous way, has accounted for Vanna. Julie herself was frightened but unhurt. The hoop came off the worst of the lot. It'll never be a hoop any more."

"Well! Can you beat it?" demanded Cornelia. "But how did *you* come into it, Polly? I guess you weren't anywhere on the scene or it would have ended long before ever they got to an accident."

"It would—I'd have seen to that all right," said Polly grimly. "*I* came into it thanks to Nancy Chester, who seems to have been holding another hoop further down the course. She tried to beat her young cousin at bowling, and then fled to find someone to come and help. *I* was the someone."

The prefects were silent a moment. Then Robin spoke.

"On the whole it seems to be just as well that Mrs Ozanne is unlikely to get to school for a week or so," she said thoughtfully. "Joey told me this morning that Mrs Chester is going on quite well, and the new baby is a darling—so Mrs Lucy says—but Mrs Ozanne won't want to leave them for a few days."

"Do you know what the baby is to be called?" asked Violet with interest.

"Mrs Lucy says she's to be Janice for herself and Mrs Chester's mother, and Agatha for Mrs Lucy's own mother. You know Mrs Ozanne and Mrs Chester are really her stepsisters, don't you? But Mrs Temple, Mrs Lucy's mother, was very good to them when they were little girls. So the baby is to have her name."

"That's very sweet of Mrs Chester—but then she *is* a sweet woman," said Violet. "Aren't there a crowd of the Chesters, though? Beth, and Nancy, and the twins, and poor little Barbara, and now this baby."

"And Paul, who comes between Beth and Nancy, and poor little Piers who died when he was only a month old," added Robin, who knew all about it, as Mrs Chester and Mrs Russell were close friends. "There've been eight of them altogether."

"It is like a book by Charlotte Yonge," laughed Yvette Mercier. "But what more about the Fourth, Polly?"

Polly grimaced, and shook herself. "Oh, they're always cheeky—"

"What else do you expect with Betty Wynne-Davies and Elizabeth Arnett in the form?" interrupted Robin.

"Nothing, my child. It would take a whole covey of archangels to look after the manners and morals of that pair. But I must say I think they've over-stepped the mark this time—and with Bill of all people!"

"Why, what *have* they said?" demanded Sigrid Björnesson, usually a very silent person.

"Well, it appears that when they were getting ready for science, Bill opened by giving them a dissertation on the general properties of gases. Betty—who certainly doesn't lack courage, even if it's wrongly applied—remarked in *anything* but an undertone to Elizabeth, 'I don't call this patriotic science at all. Why on earth can't she yarn about the properties of the soil if yarn she must?' Bill heard her— I believe she was meant to—and the resultant row seems to have been an outsize row.''

"But who told you all this?" demanded Robin. "Not Bill, surely?"

"*Bill*? My dear Rob, have you lost your wits? I got it from Biddy O'Ryan and Mary Shaw when I went to tick the form off for talking on the stairs. I missed those two, and wanted to know where they were, and was informed that they were in the punishment room with Bill—and why."

"Betty Wynne-Davies really is the limit!" observed Cornelia. "She gets worse instead of better if you ask me."

Robin began to laugh. "I remember when we first joined up with the Saints—doesn't it seem centuries ago?—that Hilary Burn told Jo that Elizabeth Arnett *thought* of the things, and Betty *did* them—with frills on!"

"It wasn't Hilary who said that; it was Ida Reaveley," said Cornelia. "Not that it really matters. The *principle's* the same. That was three years ago this term, and they haven't improved a scrap. They were eleven then, and they're fourteen now—nearly fifteen—and they've no more sense than—than the Ozanne twins and the rest of that crowd."

"What lovely Seniors they seem likely to make!" ejaculated Yvette. "What *will* become of the school if it's left to characters like that?"

"Oh, they'll learn sense in time, " said Sigrid comfortably. "Look at us! We weren't little angels by any means. We played up in our time and I'm sure we're as responsible as most prees nowadays—rather more so, in fact."

"We've got more reason to be," Cornelia reminded her. "All the same, you're right in some ways, Sigrid. I know *I* was a regular little beast when I first came to school. I only wonder they ever put up with me. But Mademoiselle—" She stopped, and the other girls, exchanging looks of sympathy, hastened to change the subject. For Mademoiselle Lepâttre, who had been Head after Mrs Russell's marriage, had given motherless Cornelia most of her mothering, and the Head Girl had felt her death during the Christmas term more than any of them.

"Well, we must do what we can to bring those imps into line," said Violet seriously. "The worst of it is I don't really know what we *can* do. I wish Joey weren't so busy these days."

"Joey is never too busy to be interested in school," said Robin quickly. "She said she hoped to be able to get up next week. Suppose we call a prefects' meeting for that day, and invite her to join us."

"That's an idea—and about our best bet, I guess," agreed Cornelia. "In the meantime, it's up to us to watch them, and see that they don't go beyond the limit."

"If we can," put in Yvette. "But you know how hard it is, Corney. We may think we have guarded all points, and then they will do something we never thought about."

This was so true that no one could think of anything to say. However, the sound of flying steps, punctuated by outbursts of wild laughter, turned their thoughts, and they all looked up with interest as the door flew open, and the three remaining members of the Sixth entered, breathless and giggling, so that at first no one could get any sense out of them. However, when they had been accommodated with chairs, they managed to pull themselves together, and Cornelia promptly demanded the reason for their mirth.

"It's the evacuees—those at the Rossers'," said Gwladys Evans, a former Braemar House girl.

"What have they been doing now?" asked Robin curiously.

"Well, you know the Rossers took two little boys from London—one's seven, and the other five?"

"Yes, I know. And one of them came tearing in from the poultry yard the other day with a new-laid egg in his hand, and told Mrs Rosser that the hens were marvellous—they laid the eggs *already cooked*!" replied Polly with a chuckle.

"This beats that," declared Iris Stephens, another new girl.

"I should think it did! Just you listen to this!" Gwladys went off into another volley of giggles, in which she was joined by Iris, and even the somewhat stately Vicky McNab.

"Oh, get on with it—do!" exclaimed Polly. "I'll shake you in a minute if you go on like that, Gwladys."

Gwladys made an effort, and became grave. "Well, Mr Rosser was taking the kids round the place, and in the orchard they came across one of those famous white sows of his—ringed, of course. You know how they bark the trees if they're not."

The prefects nodded. They did indeed know, having had a demonstration of this fact when Betty Wynne-Davies and Biddy O'Ryan had left the orchard gate open, and a young pig had got in and stripped the bark from several apple-trees before it was found out. The resultant lecture the school at large had received on the iniquity of leaving gates open in the country had never been bettered by Miss Annersley, and even the heedless Fourth had contrived to shut all gates after them ever since.

"Well," went on Gwladys, who was rather addicted to this opening gambit, "the small boy wanted to know why the piggy had a ring through its nose. Before Mr Rosser could say anything, he got his answer—from his brother. 'Don't yer know *thet*? Thet's becorse it's *married*, of course!' "

The Sixth shrieked in unison at this unexpected explanation. The evacuees at the farms and cottages round about were responsible for a good deal of the laughter just at present, for most of them were city children who, coming from poor areas, knew nothing about the country, and their comments were unconsciously humorous in the extreme.

Robin proceeded to try to cap the tale. "You know Griffiths-the-Home-Farm?" she began, using the Welsh description given by most folk of the district. "Well, they have a small girl of seven or eight. One of their sheep had three lambs this year, so one of them had to be fed by bottle. It became a great pet, and a regular nuisance, so Joey says; used to trot up to everyone, expecting a nice bottle as soon as they appeared. Well, one day this poor kiddy came tearing into the kitchen, yelling at the top of her voice, and plainly terrified. Mrs Griffiths tried to find out what was the matter, and the poor little soul sobbed out that she had been chased by a wild animal, and she wanted to go home. At first Mrs Griffiths wondered if it could be one of the sheepdogs, and she went out to see, for she'd thought they were all away that day. There wasn't any sheepdog there. But Bobby—that's the lamb—was wandering round, and when he saw her, he ran baaing to her. The kiddy heard him, and yelled, 'That's him! He's *roaring* at you! Do come in or he'll *eat* you!' Bobby had gone to her for his bottle!''

Again the girls laughed. Then they sobered. ''Doesn't it seem awful?'' said Vicky. ''Fancy children reaching the ages of six and seven and knowing no better!''

''They'll know better when they do go back home,'' said Polly. ''Still, you're right, Vicky. It *is* all wrong that they should have such ideas.''

''And they are so pathetic over the flowers,'' added Violet. ''Miss Denny was telling me yesterday that she was stopped by two little girls. She had been gathering milk-maids from the ditch, and they told her the 'Park-keeper' would be after her if she did things like that. The poor mites had never seen flowers except in the public parks where it says 'Keep off the grass', and they *are* chased if they try to pick the flowers. She soon put them right, and they went home clutching big bunches of milkmaids and cowslips.''

Robin sat up suddenly. ''Look here,'' she said, ''we talk a good deal about these children, and say how sorry we are for them. Let's *do* something, as well as talk.''

''What do you want to do?'' asked Cornelia.

''Let's ask permission to have a party for them—some of them, anyhow—and give them as good a time as we can. I'm sure we could give them a picnic tea in the meadow.

And there are heaps of milkmaids and cowslips and other kinds of flowers, too, growing there. And we could take them round the farm part, and show them the animals.''

"And all subscribe, and have races, and give them prizes. Oh yes, it's a great idea, Rob! Let's do it!'' cried Violet.

"We'll go to the Abbess and see what she says first, I guess,'' said Cornelia. "She mightn't altogether like it. Grown-ups are so afraid of measles, and mumps, and things like that.''

"Oh, they aren't likely to have them just now. *This* isn't the term for that sort of thing,'' said Polly easily. "Still, it might be just as well to see what the staff think before we tackle the rest of the school. All right, Corney. We'll go along after supper and see what she thinks about it. And there's the gong for tea, and I'm ready for it, I can tell you. Come along, you folk! It's rude to keep people waiting!''

CHAPTER 11

Joey Takes A Hand

Joey Maynard, toiling up the steep drive to Plas Howell, paused to mop her hot face and wish aloud that she could reach her destination without the trouble of getting there. As she had the pram containing the precious triplets with her, there is less reason to be surprised at her discontent. In addition, the fiat of the Government that all aliens, whether friendly or otherwise, must be interned had robbed her of her close friend, Frieda von Ahlen, once Frieda Mensch. The latter had departed for the Isle of Man only the previous day, and Joey was missing her badly.

"It's such nonsense!" she thought rebelliously as she went on, pushing the big pram before her. "Poor Frieda has reason enough to hate every Nazi with a deadly hatred. They've lost almost everything they possess; and then there was all that Bruno had to suffer in that horrible concentration camp! And he's fighting in the Polish Legion, so I think the Government might have let Frieda alone."

A shout of "Joey! Ahoy!" turned her thoughts, and made her look along the narrow path which ran out into the drive at this point. Racing down it were Daisy Venables, followed by Beth and Gwensi. These three had made a firm alliance already. Daisy and Beth had been good friends for nearly a year now; and they had taken Gwensi in quite cheerfully. Joey, waiting for the trio, noted that the small girl's face was pink and beaming with smiles, and her big dark eyes had lost their desolate look.

"Good for Beth and Daisy!" thought the elder girl. Then they were on her, and Beth and Gwensi were hanging over the pram, exclaiming at the way the triplets had grown in the three weeks which had passed since they had last seen them; while Daisy had fallen on her, and was hugging her as if they had been parted for three months instead of only three days. Joey had sent Daisy and Robin up to school to board from the Monday, since she wanted Frieda's last days to herself.

Leaving the pram to the tender mercies of Beth and Gwensi, Joey took long-legged Daisy into her arms and hugged her. "Daisy-girl! What a wild and woolly object you look in that kit! Is it your day for gardening?"

"Yes! We saw you coming through the trees and asked Evvy if we might come to meet you and bring you to look at our garden, and she said yes. Come along and see what we've done!"

"Can I wheel the pram, please?" begged Gwensi. "Do let me, Mrs Maynard! I'll be ever so careful."

"All right. Don't tip it over—that's all I ask," responded Jo easily. "Daisy, Frieda sent you her love, and she hopes to be back before too long. I don't expect they'll keep her very long. After all, Bruno *is* fighting for us."

"I can't see why Frieda should be sent away at all," said Daisy as she clung to Jo's arm. "*She*'s not an enemy!"

"I suppose they can't begin letting one person here and there off, or they'd never be able to end," said Jo with a sigh. "But it *is* hard lines. I'm very glad Bernie and Kurt are in America, and Tante Gretchen and Onkel Reise with them. And they're leaving Maria and Frau Marani alone, I'm thankful to say. Also Gisela and Gottfried. That's what I can't understand—why they should leave Gottfried and take Frieda, who is his sister."

"Oh, have there been letters from Guernsey, then?" cried Beth, who had overheard all this.

"Yes, this morning. By the way, Bethy, you are to come home with Rob and Daisy on Friday, and on Saturday we are all going to see the new baby. Your Aunt Janie rang me up this morning, and she says your mother is much better and able to have visitors now."

Beth's violet eyes widened. "Really? No one ever told me."

"No one could, for we only knew this morning," returned Joey briskly. She knew, for little Mrs Lucy had

95

confided in her, that there had been bad trouble with Beth over her youngest sister, Barbara. Born at a time when Dr Chester had had severe money losses, Barbara had been terribly fragile, and Mrs Chester had absorbed herself in saving the life of the frail baby who was all the dearer for her fragility. Beth, old enough to feel the change in their circumstances, and to resent it without realizing what a grief it was to her parents, imagined herself neglected for the new little sister, and had been almost fiercely jealous.

To make matters worse, while the brother next to her in age was sent by his godfather Mr Ozanne to a good preparatory school with his cousins, the Ozanne boys, Beth herself had been sent to a very second-rate private school, since the education was not bad and her parents felt they could not afford bigger fees for her. Mrs Lucy would have been glad to pay for the child at a good school, but Anne Chester was bitterly proud, and flatly refused. The younger children could share the Lucys' governess, but she frankly declared herself unable to take on any one of Beth's age. Beth, therefore, was left to feel that her parents cared less for her than for any of the others, and, at one time, this silliness had threatened to warp a character already difficult. Mercifully for all concerned, the Chalet School had begun in Guernsey, and two terms of it had made a big difference in Beth already.

Mrs Lucy had told Joey that she was afraid of how her eldest niece would take the arrival of Baby Janice, and Joey had volunteered to do what she could to ease matters. Now, as Daisy rushed on to join Gwensi at the pram, she laid a hand on the other child's arm, and drew her to her.

"Don't *you* desert me, too, Beth. Look at those two mad creatures! Daisy and Gwensi, if you upset my precious triplets on the drive, you may take ship for the furthest place from here. Remember that!"

Daisy and Gwensi, who had been harnessing themselves by means of belts to the pram, decided to give it up, and revert to the tried method of pushing, while Jo, with an arm

96

round Beth's slim shoulders, strolled after them, intent on fulfilling her promise to Janie Lucy.

"Aren't you longing to see her, Beth? Your Aunt Janie says she's a lovely baby, with a mop of fine black hair, and very dark blue eyes."

"Not in the least like the rest of us, then," said Beth thoughtfully. "Nancy is the darkest of us, and she has only brown hair and brown eyes."

"Oh, Nancy isn't really *dark*," said Joey. "Paul is nearer that than the rest of you. And, of course, the baby's hair may come off and come in fair. But I do think her eyes will be very deep brown. Of course, all babies are born with more or less blue eyes."

Beth turned an incredulous look on her. "Oh, Mrs Maynard, not *really*?"

"Yes—really. Just like puppies or kittens. Look at my triplets. Len's eyes will be grey, and I'm certain Margot's will remain blue. But Connie's have changed already. If they're not black like mine, they'll be at least as dark as young David's."

Beth laughed. "How weird! I didn't know that. Oh, I do hope it'll be all right and we *can* see Mummy on Saturday. I'd like to see the new baby."

"So *that's* all right," thought Joey with an inward sigh of relief, and turned her attention to the big beds which they had now reached. "You do seem to have done a lot in a very short time, you people. Oh, good afternoon, Miss Everett; how well you've all got on with the gardens! I can just stay to admire them for two minutes, and then I must get on to the house. The prefects are expecting me at three."

"What for?" asked Daisy suspiciously.

"To decide whether you people are to be spanked for your evil deeds or given extra lessons," returned Jo calmly.

A howl of indignation arose at this, and she chuckled to herself as she perambulated round the beds, admiring all that had been done. The girls had worked hard, and rows of string, and pegs with labels attached, showed where the various crops were sown. The Third were devoting their garden mainly to salads, and had put in various kinds of lettuce, radishes, mustard and cress, chives, chicory, onions, and endive. Later, when all fear of late frosts was over, they planned to have tomatoes, and already the sturdy little plants were hardening off in the cold frame, under the care of the Sixth. Right at the back of everything, some thrifty gooseberry bushes of three or four years' growth had been pruned and brought into proper bearing condition. Gwensi pointed them out eagerly, explaining that Evan Evans had risked upsetting them, and planted them out before the girls had come, so that the young ladies might have some fruit that very summer.

"And Beth is putting strawberry runners round the edge," said Miss Everett. "Daisy and Gwensi are helping her, and they are managing very well, so we may hope for some strawberries later on."

"Mercy on us!" exclaimed Jo in surprise. "Will they give fruit the very year they are planted?"

"Yes, if they've been struck the previous year," said Miss Everett.

"*Struck*? What *do* you mean?" demanded her visitor, who was almost blankly ignorant of everything to do with gardens. "Have you to thrash them as I've always been led to understand you must thrash walnuts if you want a good crop?"

Giggles from the girls and a grin from Miss Everett answered this innocent question.

Jo looked at them in haughty surprise, which became a giggle as she realized that she had said something absurd. "Well! What have I said?" she demanded. "Evidently it's something idiotic. Hurry up and tell me, for I must go, or the prees will all be on my track!"

"When you 'strike' a plant, Mrs Maynard," explained Miss Everett, "you plant a cutting, or, in the case of strawberries, a runner—that is a prostrate shoot which makes roots at the end if it gets a chance—in a thumb-pot—or the earth, as the case may be, and let it make roots."

"Oh, I see." Joey strolled towards the pram where her

daughters were sleeping peacefully. "Well, it's all frightfully interesting, and I congratulate you all on the work you're doing. But now I must get on. By the way, one last question: why the straw along the strawberries?"

"Partly to be a protection in case of frosts, and also partly to keep the fruit clean of soil if we have a wet summer. At the end of the season, the straw will be raked off, the weeds cleared away, and the new runners cut away. Then we fork well round the plants, and we should have a fine crop next year. We are going to net them this year, for birds are the most awful thieves. *And* we shall all have to go slug-hunting in the evenings, for slugs are even worse." Miss Everett wound up her discourse with another grin at the girls, who grinned back.

"What a business! Well, I'm sorry, but I shan't have time. Between babies, housekeeping, and my new book, my time is very well occupied. The garden will have to be left to Griffith Griffiths. Goodbye, you people. I really am going this time." And Joey turned the pram, and pushed it vigorously away in the direction of the house, where seven impatient people were awaiting her, and watching for her from the wide, grassy terrace which ran round three sides of it.

Robin saw her first, and went racing over the newly-mown grass to meet her. The rest were not far behind. Jo stopped the pram, drew it into the side, and, to quote herself, "stood by to repel boarders."

"Steady, you people," she remarked; "don't wake the children, whatever you do. They're due to sleep another half-hour, and if they are disturbed, they're apt to be peevish about it."

The seven moderated their raptures at this, and presently Jo, having greeted them all, turned to the pram, and carefully lifted out one baby after another, handing them to Robin, Cornelia, and Polly, who received them with much pride. The pram was drawn into shelter, under a huge oak tree, and then the party entered the house and made for the prefects' room, where the triplets were, at their mother's suggestion, ensconced in a huge old armchair, well fenced in with cushions, and left to finish their nap.

"Well," said Jo, when all this had been attended to, "why all the anxiety to see me?"

"We want advice," returned Polly.

"I gathered that. What is it about this time?"

"The Middles—what else? I guess you know as well as I do that when there's violent need of seasoned advice it always *is* the Middles," declared Cornelia.

Jo frowned. "Which Middles?" she enquired; "I thought the Thirds seemed rather a jolly set this year."

"So they are. Oh, if all Middles had no more sin to their record than the Thirds, life would be easy enough. It's more than can be said for the Fourth, though," said Robin.

Jo uttered an exclamation of impatience. "It always *is* the Fourth! What can it be about a Fourth Form that makes the gentlest and quietest of them all behave like a young demon once she enters it?"

"It's not the form—it's the age, I guess," said Cornelia. "Think what *we* were like at fourteen, Joey—not to mention your noble self."

"That's a libel on my beautiful character," retorted Joey.

"*Your* beautiful character!" jeered Cornelia. "Why, from all accounts you kept the school in a perfect ferment most of the time!"

Jo laughed self-consciously. "Touché! Oh, I admit I wasn't a little archangel by any means! Still, I don't think our crowd were ever as hair-raising as yours, Cornelia, my love. Well, let's get down to brass tacks—"

"Do you know, Joey, you've got into a habit of beginning every other sentence with 'well'?" interrupted Polly Heriot with interest. "Is this the latest development?"

"I'm sure I don't!" said Joey indignantly.

"You do, though, Joey," Robin put in. "I've noticed it."

"Have you indeed? Well, never mind me. Tell me what the Fourths have been up to lately—and hurry up about it. It's after half-past three, and more than time for the babes to wake up."

They came to business immediately.

"It began with Biddy O'Ryan," said Cornelia. "You know we all wear corduroys and pullovers for gardening? Well, one day, when it *wasn't* their day for the garden—I mean for Miss Everett, of course—Biddy marched down to breakfast in her gardening kit. Naturally she was ticked off—I saw to that part myself—and sent back to change."

"Good job, too. What was the idea?"

"We found that out later. The next afternoon, when the Abbess was showing round some rather important visitors—or so we gathered—Betty Wynne-Davies and Elizabeth Arnett put in an appearance in front of the house—"

"Where they'd no right to be," interjected Polly.

"Exactly! Where they'd no possible right to be, looking like a pair of ragamuffins, in *their* corduroys and pullovers. As the Abbess had just been exhibiting the gardens where it was the Seconds' turn, and where they had all been working as good as gold, she knew well enough that those two young *minxes* had no more right than she to be in such kit at that time. She couldn't say anything, of course, but I guess she thought plenty. And then, when they got up to her party, she made the pleasing discovery that the pair of them had been using *lipstick*!"

"*What?*"

"Pillar box red, at that," put in Sigrid. "You could see it a mile away, judging by what she said to us later."

"Well, I must say I think it's the limit of them," said Jo stormily. "Were they out to get the school a bad name, or what?"

"Not they! I don't believe they'd ever thought of that side of it. She had them into her room later, and wiped up the floor with them. It was rather a pity that Bill had met them twenty minutes earlier, and put in some good work on the subject at the time. They were both pretty mad—you know what Bill's tongue can be!—and the Abbess hauling them over the coals put their backs well up."

"What happened?"

"Well, if one can rely on what Betty tells, she said, 'We were only trying to show them how up-to-date the school is, Miss Annersley'."

"I don't believe it!" said Jo decisively. "Not even Betty Wynne-Davies has the cheek for that!"

"She stuck to it that she did—and Elizabeth backed her up in it," said Polly.

"Oh, rats! They were pulling your legs! We—however, I mean, let's go on. Is there much more of it?"

"Reams! I guess you'll open your eyes before we're done," said Cornelia darkly.

"Oh? This sounds interesting. What was the next item on the programme?"

"Weezes, or whatever they call those awful scarf-things you tie round your head," said Polly. "They all broke out in them at once—and nice frights they all looked. It was their gardening day, and Evvy simply gave them all one look—I was there with a message from the Abbess, so I saw it—and then said, 'You vulgar little sights! Go and take off those disgusting things at once, and don't dare to come to me looking like that again!' They went—with Evvy looking like that, they couldn't do anything else.

"I can quite imagine it! So the Fourth have decided to come over all modish and up-to-date, have they? You'd better give me the whole yarn and let me know the worst." And Jo settled back in her chair after a glance at her babies to be sure that they were still sleeping soundly, and prepared to hear the rest of the sad tale.

"Oh, it's all of a piece!" Polly spoke impatiently. "They've tried coloured varnish for their fingernails, and Betty has been talking of getting her hair 'permed'—"

"What on earth for? I should have said nature had done it sufficiently well for her already."

"Yes, but it doesn't wave regularly—or some such rot as that!"

"I see. Well, if she ever *does* get it permed, she'll live to regret it—I can tell her that."

102

"They use powder—I am sure of it," Jeanne de Marné spoke up in her soft voice.

"Oh, so am I," agreed Cornelia, "though I've never caught them at it. And they're generally going the right way to spoil the rest. It's all Betty and Elizabeth, of course. The little asses have got it into their heads that they must begin to think about their appearances, and they're well on the way to making themselves look like the cheapest of the cheap!"

"But," said Joey, "surely the Abbess won't allow that sort of thing to go on. I mean, there'll be rules about it, won't there?"

"Rather! Rules made that very night—I mean the one after the lipstick affair—and we were all fetched into Hall and told just how horrid it was in 'mere schoolgirls'!" quoted Polly cheerfully.

"Then I don't see why you are worrying."

"*Don't* you? That's not like you, Jo. Don't you see that if they've started making themselves cheap in one direction they won't stop at it; they'll be cheap in others. And the worst of it is, it isn't only themselves we have to worry over. We've got to face it—Betty and Elizabeth are leaders all right, and they do set the tone for that form. If—"

Cornelia never finished her remarks. Without warning, the door burst open, and Monica Marilliar bounced in to exclaim breathlessly, "You've all got to go down to Hall— Miss Annersley says so. There are police here, and some soldiers, and there's going to be a most *awful* row! I've been sent for you, and the rest of the school is to be hauled in too. Better come at once!" Then she turned, and vanished as precipitately as she had come.

The prefects leapt to their feet, pushing back their chairs with small regard for the slumbers of the triplets, who, rudely awakened in such a fashion, set up three separate yells that spoke well for the strength of their lungs. Joey rushed to them, while the girls, unheeding the three for the first time since their arrival into the world, hurried out after Monica without more ado.

"Oh, drat—*drat*—DRAT!" ejaculated Joey as she began to try to soothe her family. "*Will* you stop crying, you there? I want to know the meaning of all this, and I want to know it pronto, as Corney used to say. Here, here's your bottles. Now then, drink up, and let's have a little peace! But what *has* happened?"

CHAPTER 12

"Who is Responsible?"

Into the Assembly Hall which had formerly been the drawing-room of Plas Howell streamed the girls from every part of the school. The only ones who were not there were the Kindergarten, for it was considered that they were too small to know anything about the question. The Sixth, hurrying in with as much dignity as they could assume after their wild flight down the stairs, found most of the Fifth already present; the majority of the Fourth; and the Second. The Third Form, being busy in the garden, had not yet arrived. One or two of the staff were standing in a little group near the dais talking earnestly together. Miss Lecoutier looked up as the Seniors entered, and gave them a curt order to go to their usual places, and they took them, casting wondering glances at each other.

Nobody dared to speak a word—the staff looked too grim for anyone to venture; but impudent Betty Wynne-Davies grimaced across at Elizabeth Arnett, who grimaced back, and only resumed her normal expression in time, for Miss Linton turned round a bare second later. Luckily for the pair, by that time they were standing looking straight ahead, and the young mistress saw nothing amiss with either of them.

Three minutes after, the Third arrived in charge of Miss Everett, followed by Monica Marilliar, who looked distinctly dishevelled by her mad rush round the building. As she passed Vicky McNab, her cousin, to go to her place with the Fifth, the latter leaned towards her and murmured something, at which Monica put up a hasty hand and smoothed her hair down. More she could not do, for Bill had entered, and was looking severely along the lines of girls. She was followed a moment later by Mrs Russell, who wore a worried look, Miss Annersley, and a big, red-faced man in the uniform of a Colonel.

"You may sit down, girls," said the Head when she had

taken her place before the reading desk. The school sat down, and fixed its eyes on the group before it.

The Head looked back at them. Then she proceeded: "Colonel Black has something to say to you all. I hope if anyone has been playing any silly tricks, she will own up to it at once, and so set our minds at rest. Believe me, girls, this is a serious matter, and if anyone—*anyone*—can throw any light on it, it is her duty as a patriot to tell us *at once*!"

She sat down, and Colonel Black stood up. "H'm! Your Head Mistress has told you that I want some information from you. I want to know if any of you have been playing tricks with torches anywhere about the grounds after dark?"

The girls stared at him. What sort of supervision did he think they had in the school?—a question which Miss Annersley had asked him point-blank when he had first told her what he wanted.

"Well?" he said, when the silence had become oppressive; "d'ye know anything about it, any of you?"

As Head Girl, Cornelia took it upon herself to reply. "Guess not," she told him, her American accent at its most marked. "It doesn't get dark all that early nowadays, and most of us are in bed before it *is* dark. And anyway, if you think any of *us* would be as mad as all that amounts to, you're mistaken."

The mounting indignation in her voice caused the Head to throw her a warning look, and she stopped speaking and sat down, her cheeks flushed, and her eyes bright with anger.

"Thank you, young lady," said the Colonel brusquely. "But can you answer for it that once you *are* all in bed you all *stay* there?"

Cornelia shook her head stubbornly. "We haven't been doing any mad things like playing with lights after blackout," she assured him. "Anyhow, it doesn't come till after all of us are in bed mostly."

The Colonel nodded. "I know that. But—I remember from my own schooldays—people have been known to get

106

up after lights-out, and—er—indulge in various pranks. If any of you girls"—he turned from her and spoke to the school at large—"have been doing such a thing, I hope you'll own up."

No one stirred. Even Betty and Elizabeth, imps of mischief as a rule, had clear consciences on this occasion. So the Colonel gazed at the school, and the school gazed back at him in silence for a few moments. Then Miss Annersley spoke.

"I think you may take that as final, Colonel," she said gravely. "I do not say that our girls are all angels, but I have never known one of them behave dishonourably, especially in a matter of such vital importance to the welfare of the country."

But the Colonel's face had grown grimmer. "Do you realize what this means, Madam? If the girls are not to blame, then I must question the rest of your household. If we cannot find the criminal there, then we must set a watch on the grounds."

Miss Annersley's face grew grim also, for she fully realized what *that* would mean. If soldiers were at large in the grounds, the girls must be kept very strictly to quarters. It would be a nuisance but it could not be helped. The work entailed on herself and the staff would be greatly increased—at any rate, until the person responsible for the showing of lights was caught. Well, it must be so. But inwardly, she was furious. Mrs Russell was wildly indignant too. Had they suffered all they had done during their last weeks in the Tyrol to meet with trouble of this kind in England?

"Is it absolutely necessary, Colonel?" she asked.

"Absolutely!" he barked at her.

It was at this point that the door opened, and Joey, bearing her usual burden of three babies, entered. The gallant Colonel stared at the tall, dark girl with the red-haired mites in her arms as if he wondered if he could believe his eyes. But Joey was accustomed to this, and was not one whit abashed. Advancing in her usual insouciant manner, she smiled widely at the assembly, and remarked, "Sorry I'm late, everyone. The family required instant attention to its wants. I came as soon as I could."

This bland speech had the effect of relaxing the feeling of strain which had been steadily growing, and there was a little rustle as Jo dropped one baby into Miss Wilson's arms; handed a second to her sister; and then took the sole remaining seat with the third cuddled up against her shoulder.

Feeling the Colonel's eyes on her, Mrs Russell made a dive after her self-possession; and, rocking a now drowsy Connie to her, introduced Jo to him, feeling inwardly that she would dearly have loved to smack the girl. "My sister, Mrs Maynard, who is an old girl of the school." She left the Colonel's name and status out of it in her agitation, and Jo grinned as impishly as even Betty Wynne-Davies could have done.

"You all look very official. What is the fuss about this time?"

Recovering his self-possession with a gasp, the Colonel told her curtly what had happened, and Jo's black eyes widened at the information.

"Spies *again*!" she exclaimed. "Are we ever to be free from them? We had that little sneak of a Hermann Eiser at the Sonnalpe. In Guernsey we were landed with that young Nazi, Gertrud Becker—though she did jack the whole thing up, poor babe!—and now it looks rather as though we were to be cursed with the same experience here. Have you any ideas on the subject, Colonel—or should it be *General*?"

"Only Colonel so far, thank you, Mrs Maynard," he answered. "But what is all this about a young Nazi in Guernsey? I haven't heard of it before." And he cast an indignant look at the Head.

Equally indignant with Jo for blurting out the information which she had intended to give to him privately, Miss Annersley replied with even more than her usual dignity. "Last term we were sent a schoolgirl whose name was given to us as Gertrude Beck, Colonel Black. As events proved

108

she was really Gertrud Becker, a Nazi who was introduced into the school because it was thought that we must possess some vital information, owing to our having been in the Tyrol so long. As Mrs Maynard has informed you, she soon regretted her attempted activities, and tried to get back to Germany. Fortunately for her, the ship in which she escaped was torpedoed, and she and some of the men were rescued by one of our destroyers which also accounted for the submarine, I believe. At first it was thought that she would be returned to us; but finally it was decided that she would be safer in other hands so she is, at present, in Scotland somewhere. The poor child was trying to reach her mother, of whom little or nothing has been heard. We all know what vengeance the Gestapo take on the friends and relatives of those who fail them," she added.

"And this girl is not among you ?" persisted the Colonel.

"No, she has never come back. We sent all her clothes and other possessions to an address given us at the time, and we have heard very little since, as I told you." Miss Annersley was beginning to lose her temper.

The Colonel was silent for a moment, pondering this information. Then he seemed to make up his mind. "I see. Well, Madam, I am sorry to put you to the trouble but, in the circumstances, I must ask that each girl come forward in turn and be asked directly if she knows anything whatsoever about this affair. If we can gain nothing from that, then I must interview the remainder of your establishment. Perhaps you would give orders to have them assembled somewhere in readiness while I attend to the matter in hand."

"Certainly," replied the Head, at her very stateliest. "Miss Wilson, would you please see to it that all the domestic staff are assembled in the servants' hall at once. Is it your wish to speak to the Kindergarten also, Colonel? I have not had them summoned as they are all under eight, and it is practically impossible for any of them to leave their dormitories without being found out."

"Can't leave one out," he replied. "I'll see them later, if you have no objection."

Miss Annersley had every objection. Some of the small folk were nervous little people, and she did not want them upset by this big, red-faced man, with his habit of barking out his words. However, she knew that she could do nothing but agree, so she turned to Gillian Linton.

"Miss Linton, would you please ask Miss Phipps to have all the little ones together in the Kindergarten room in an hour's time? We will see them there, I think."

Gillian Linton rose obediently. "Yes, Miss Annersley. They are playing in the meadow. Shall I ask Miss Phipps to bring them in at once?"

Miss Annersley considered. "No, I think they may have another three-quarters of an hour. But you might ask Miss Dene to ring up Mrs Ozanne, Mrs Lucy, and any other parents of day-children, and explain that the children will be a little later today, but we will see that they are brought safely home." She glanced at Colonel Black as she finished speaking, but he said nothing. Gillian departed on her errand, and the individual questioning began.

One by one the girls marched up to the dais, to be asked, "Have you anything to do with this signalling, or do you know anything about it?"

One by one the girls looked the questioner in the face, and said, "No, nothing!" Some spoke indignantly; one or two sounded frightened. Biddy O'Ryan created a minor sensation by reverting to creamiest Kerry brogue when she answered, "Sorra wan thing do Oi know av ut, yer Honour!" Whereat the Colonel, under the impression that she was making fun of him, glared awfully at her, and Miss Lecoutier made a mental note to give the young lady a good talking-to on the subject of speaking good English.

When finally the baby of the Second—little Primula Venables—had returned to her place, they were no further forward. Everyone had denied knowing anything about it.

Miss Annersley turned to her guest. "Have you finished with my pupils, Colonel? If so, I will dismiss them, and they may go back to their lessons. Ah"—as the chiming of the clock interrupted her—"It is four o'clock already."

"I'll just hear what these young ladies have to say," returned the exasperated Colonel, who would have soon tackled any number of men, but who felt like a fish out of water in a girls' school, and who had, by this time, come to the conclusion that every member of it was laughing at him. He indicated the staff with a wave of his hand.

"Certainly," agreed the Head. "Miss Wilson"—for that lady had returned, having left the rounding-up of the domestic staff in the capable hands of Megan—"would you please answer the Colonel's question."

So, one by one, the staff, too, made their denials; and then, having roused Miss Annersley to a pitch of fury as she had rarely felt before, and all connected with the school to a sense of wild indignation that anyone could refuse to take their collective word, he told the Head curtly that he was finished with them for the present, and ready to interview the servants.

Then—"Trust Jo to throw a monkey-wrench in the works!" as Cornelia feelingly remarked later on—that young lady turned her most limpidly guileless glance on the Colonel, and observed: "You have not questioned *me*, Colonel—nor my sister. We are part of the school, you know. I am afraid my babies are not able to express themselves coherently as yet, but perhaps you would take my assurance on their behalf that neither they nor I have had anything to do with it."

A splutter—instantly suppressed—sounded from the direction of the Fourth, who fully appreciated this. The Colonel turned deeply purple but, perhaps mercifully, seemed at a loss for words. Mrs Russell hastily spoke up in a noble endeavour to smooth things over. "You must forgive my sister, Colonel. She isn't very many years from her own schooldays, even yet; and—and—" She faltered and ceased, having encountered a look so appalling from Jo that she was momentarily thrown off her balance.

"What on earth did you want to blather like that for?" demanded the latter young lady later on.

"Because he was mad enough without *you* making things

111

worse!" retorted Madge Russell severely. "Really, Jo, considering you're a married woman and the mother of a family, I must say you haven't much sense!"

"I *meant* to madden him," was Jo's unchristian remark. "He had a nerve, I must say, to go questioning the girls like that, let alone the staff! What does he take us for? I don't believe he's an Englishman at all! He's a wretched Nazi dressed up in our uniform, going round to make people discontented with the Government. I've heard they did that sort of thing in the last war."

"If you go broadcasting scandalous statements of that kind you'll find yourself one of the chief figures in a libel action," returned Madge. "For Heaven's sake hold your tongue and try to develop a little common sense, Josephine!"

But Joey was not heeding her. "You told him I wasn't so many years from my own schooldays," she said thoughtfully. "Do you realize that you were right? It's five years in July since I left school as a pupil. I went back the next term, you may remember, because of the measles business. Mademoiselle was taken ill that term, and I stayed to teach. D'you remember, Madge! What hundreds of things have happened since then! The Saints and the Chalet joined up; we had to leave the Tyrol—I still dream of that when I have nightmares—and the school was closed for a year. Josette arrived, and I got married. The school opened again in Guernsey, and my triplets arrived. Frieda married Bruno von Ahlen. We had to clear out of Guernsey and come here. Frieda is interned, and goodness knows when they'll let her come back! *Now* we're landed with a spy hunt! But what I should like to know is who is it?"

And that, in effect, was what the entire school was asking.

CHAPTER 13

The Fourth Decides to Take a Hand

"We've got to do something about it!" The speaker was Betty Wynne-Davies, and she was on her favourite perch—the big garden roller. How she ever managed to maintain her balance as she did was a mystery to most folk, for she was rarely still an instant, and the majority of people would find it hard enough to stand still in such a place without falling off whereas Betty "dickey-danced", to quote Polly Heriot's graphic phrase, the whole time.

"It's all very well talking," said Nicole de Saumarez, "but what *can* we do?"

Needless to state, they were talking about the latest excitement. The whole school had been brought to boiling point by the affair. None of the domestic staff owned to knowing anything about the mysterious lights which had been appearing in the woods, and, as a result, Colonel Black had insisted on posting soldiers at various points in and about the grounds from five o'clock in the evening onwards. This had curtailed the girls' liberty, and they were restricted to the garden, the tennis courts, and the little paddock which ran down one side of the kitchen garden, instead of having the freedom of the whole park. What was worse, both from their point of view and the staff's, a mistress had to be on duty with them while they were out. Supervision at the Chalet School had always been as light as possible, Madge Russell preferring to rely on the sense of honour of the school to police work. Naturally the girls resented the new order of things; and the staff resented it still more, for it broke in on their comparatively scanty leisure time.

Now, Betty merely bent a glance of scorn on the Jersey girl, and went on with her speech. "It's the limit, having mistresses all over the place wherever you go. We've always been trusted, and I think it's rotten to have to have sheep-dogs after us like this. As though we were likely to mess about with lights and risk having bombs chucked at us!"

"I dare say," persisted Nicole, "but what can we really do after all? We can growl as much as we like—and I'll bet the staff do the same. But as long as that fat, red-faced ninny of a Colonel says we've got to have soldiers about the place, no one can do anything about it. It's Government orders, and if the Abbess didn't agree, they'd fine her, or imprison her—or something."

"I'll tell you what we can do." Betty bent forward, nearly going headlong into their midst, and speaking in low, mysterious tones. "We can try to catch whoever is doing it. Then, when we've caught him—"

"But it may be a her," objected her closest friend, Elizabeth.

"*Or* her, then, since you're so particular—we'll take them along to the nearest tommy and hand them over. Then they'll leave us alone, and we may get a little peace from Bill and the rest."

"You mean they may get a little peace from *us*. I reckon they can do with it, too!" retorted Mary Shand, a small American from South Carolina, whose parents had not chosen to let her take the risk of crossing the Atlantic since the outbreak of the war. "If we're sick of *them* by the end of the day, they must be mighty sick of *us*!"

"Why ever!" Nicole was honestly amazed at this idea.

Mary wagged her head knowingly. "I've heard my sister talk. She teaches history in the high school at Union near our home, and she always said she'd had more'n enough by nightfall."

"Oh, well, that's got nothing to do with this," said Elizabeth impatiently. "Dry up, you two, and let's think what we can do to catch the Spy." The Fourth, and, indeed, most of the school, spoke of the originator of the lights with a capital letter.

Thus urged, the Fourth assumed attitudes of thought, and wrestled with the problem to the best of its ability.

114

"If we could hear of any secret passages," began Nicole at last.

She got no further. "You and your secret passages! D'you think all houses in England sport them?" jeered Elizabeth.

Nicole stood her ground sturdily. "You never know. This is an old house—oldish, anyhow. It was built before the Forty-Five, didn't Mary—I mean Miss Burnett—say?" she finished hastily. Those girls who had been at school with Mary Burnett found it none too easy to remember that she must be "Miss Burnett" to them nowadays; even as they had had a hard time turning Simone Lecoutier into "Miss Lecoutier". But Miss Annersley had enforced it very strictly, and they were beginning to manage better.

"The Forty-Five, wouldn't be likely to affect this part of the world," said Elizabeth, who happened to be keen on history. "If it had been in the north of England it might have been another story. As it is, I don't believe anyone paid much attention to it."

"Still, there *might* be a hidden way somewhere," persisted Nicole. "Couldn't that kid Gwensi tell us? Why not ask her?"

"It's an idea. I'll go get her, shall I?" And Mary jumped down from the back of the garden seat on which she had been perched, and turned to leave what had once been a bowling alley, which had become the Fourth's recognized meeting-place.

"Yes, do," agreed Elizabeth. "If it does no good, it can't do any harm, anyhow. Buck up about it, do! We'll have to get back to the house for prep in twenty minutes' time."

Thus encouraged, Mary raced off, to return a few minutes later with Gwensi, Daisy, and Beth, who all looked curious as to the reason for the summons.

"Here!" protested Betty at sight of the other two; "we didn't send for you two—we only wanted Gwensi."

"Then you'll take us with her!" returned Daisy calmly. Joey Maynard had told her and Beth to look after the new child, and they were doing it with all their might. The three had become tremendous friends and were rarely seen apart. When Mary had brought the Fourth's summons, Daisy and Beth had insisted on coming with their third member to find out what it was they wanted with her. The Fourth were no friends of theirs, and Betty and Elizabeth had a reputation of being inclined to bully younger people on occasion. Therefore the two meant to keep an eye on their protégée.

Betty turned a glare on her but it had no effect, Daisy merely returning it with interest. Finally, deciding that time was slipping away, and if they meant to do anything it had better be done at once, the leader of the Fourth turned to the business in hand.

"We don't want much. We only want to know if you've ever heard of any hidden rooms or secret passages in the house," she said quite mildly.

Gwensi stared. "Secret rooms or passages? Of course there aren't."

"How d'you know?" demanded Nicole. "It's an old house. Lots of old houses have them. Didn't you once say your Aunt Janie's house in Guernsey had one, Beth?" She turned to Beth Chester.

Beth nodded. "Yes—leading to caves in the cliffs. I've never seen it. It wasn't safe, and Uncle and Auntie wouldn't let us go near the cellar where it was—it was always kept locked up. But I know it's there all right. Auntie said so."

"There you are, then. If your aunt had one, why shouldn't there be one at Plas Howell? Are you *sure* you've never heard of any, Gwensi?"

Gwensi shook her head. "Not the first murmur of a whisper of one. But I can ask Megan, if you like," she added. "She'd be sure to know."

"Oh, don't bother," said Elizabeth hastily. She had no wish for any grown-up to hear of their ideas. Megan, if questioned, would be sure to ask why they wanted to know, and Elizabeth had no idea of letting anyone older than Nicole, who happened to be the eldest in the form, into the secret.

"Why not?" demanded Daisy with interest. "You didn't

send for Gwen to ask her that for nothing, *I* know. What's at the back of it?"

"You hold your tongue!" retorted Betty, her quick temper rising. "No one asked you to butt in, Daisy Venables. You just mind your own business and let ours alone."

"Then you leave Gwensi alone. She's told you she doesn't know anything about a passage, which is why you sent for her—or so you say. You've nothing to do with what she says to her own old nurse. Come on, Gwen—come on, Beth! They don't want us any more, now they know." And with an arm through one of each of her chums, Daisy wheeled them round and marched them off, leaving the Fourth too stunned with surprise at being addressed in this way to say anything until they were gone.

But once the form had recovered, it did not spare its tongues.

"You *idiot*!" cried Elizabeth to Betty. "What did you want to go and do that for? Now that little ass of a Gwensi will go and start talking to that old Nanny of hers, and *she*'ll talk to some of the maids, and it'll get to the Abbess before you can say 'Knife!' I did think you would have a little more sense than that!"

"Oh no, she shan't! I'll see to that!" flared Betty. "And if you come to that, why didn't some of you lunatics stop those kids clearing out like that?"

"I like that! How could we?" demanded Mary, firing up. "You didn't expect us to grab the kids and hold them by main force, did you?"

As, in her temper, this was just what Betty *had* expected, she was silent. She knew well enough that all the members of her form did not altogether approve of some of her methods.

Biddy O'Ryan took up the tale in her soft sweet voice with its Irish brogue, once rich as cream, but now only faintly flavouring her talk. "It's not much we found from that. What will we do next?"

"I'll tackle Megan myself," said Betty suddenly.

"Betty! You can't! Besides, Megan won't tell you a thing."

117

"Perhaps she'll tell me more than she thinks she's doing," replied Betty darkly. "You leave it to me. I'll manage it somehow."

"I don't see how. Oh, bother! There's the bell for prep!" And Mary climbed down from her perch once more.

The rest followed her example reluctantly, but none the less promptly. Punctuality was a virtue on which much stress was laid at the Chalet School, and none of them dared disregard the summons of the bell.

It is to be feared that the Fourth did little preparation that evening. They were too busy trying to think out ways of capturing the person responsible for those lights. However, they were so absorbed that they forgot their usual practice of trying to make the hour and a half a species of purgatory for the prefect in charge; and Robin Humphries gathered up her books when it was over with a feeling of surprise that she had managed to get so much of her own work done.

"They must be reforming at long last," she decided, as she strolled through the hall and up the stairs to the prefects' room where she found her fellows still hard at work. Polly, who had just come in after a tussle with the Third, who had decided to see how many questions—quite legitimate ones, of course—they could put to her during the time, looked at her with a sympathetic glance born of a fellow-feeling, which quickly gave way to one of amazement as she noted Robin's unruffled brow and cheerful smile.

"Where have you been?" she demanded.

"With the Fourth, of course. Where do you expect?" returned Robin. "It's my night on duty with them."

"With the Fourth! Were any of them absent, by any chance?"

"Not one—why?"

"Then what's happened?"

"Nothing's happened. What *are* you driving at?"

"Well, I must say that for someone who's been taking Fourth Form prep you look uncommonly calm and collected," observed Cornelia, removing her glasses to polish them. "Were any of the staff there?"

"Not one of them. I was all by myself. As for the Fourth, they really worked tonight—or, at any rate, they were quiet. I expect Bill or someone has been hauling them over the coals, and they're feeling subdued for a while."

"*Never*!" retorted Polly with emphasis. "Not even Bill could subdue that little crowd for more than half an hour. If they have really been quiet as you say, then they must be sickening for something!"

"Not very likely. This isn't sickness term," put in Sigrid Björnesson. "Perhaps they've begun to reform after all the row they got into over their efforts to appear up-to-date and modish."

Yvonne Mercier laughed. "Oh, no, ma chére! You must think of something else. I agree with Polly. *No* row is likely to make those little nuisances good and hard-working for more than half an hour."

"I think Sigrid may be right," said Robin thoughtfully. "After all, they are growing up now. Betty is almost fifteen, isn't she? And Nicole *was* fifteen two days ago. Fifteen isn't a baby any more. Besides," she added, warming to her subject, "I'm sure all the experiences we've had lately are enough to age anyone. I don't feel nearly such an infant as I did at this time last year. Well, it's half-past seven, and time Daisy and I were off. Joey doesn't like it if we're out after eight these days."

"Can you wonder?" demanded Cornelia. "What with soldiers everywhere, and the possibility of a stray aeroplane slipping through with a bomb or two to liven things up, I only wonder she allows you to stay for prep at all."

"It's only for this term." Robin was sorting out her books as she spoke. "Next term we've got to be boarders. Weekly boarders, anyhow. Jo says she doesn't like the idea of our being out after blackout."

"The war may be over by that time," suggested Sigrid.

"I only wish it might! Joey misses Jack terribly. And since things have gone so badly in France, I know she's anxious about the Islands and Jem and the rest at the San."

At this moment Lorenz Maïco, who had been with Miss

Wilson for coaching in botany, appeared to announce that Robin was wanted on the phone, so the latter dropped her books and raced off. She returned five minutes later, and her grave face told the rest that something was badly wrong.

"What is it, Rob?" exclaimed Polly, springing up.

"Joey rang me up to tell me that they are evacuating the Islands as quickly as possible. The San patients have all been brought over to England, and most of the doctors are with them. But—Dr Jem—has stayed behind because he is head," replied Robin with a quiver in her voice. Mrs Russell's husband was her guardian with his wife, and she loved them both dearly. She could guess what Madge Russell must be feeling at this moment. Apart from that, this brought the war very much nearer to them all.

The prefects sat in stunned silence for a moment. Then, once more there came the sound of flying footsteps, and Monica Marilliar, again the bearer of startling news, came flying in. "Corney, everyone is to go to the Abbess in the garden at once!" she cried. "Gwensi Howell, Daisy Venables, and Beth Chester never came into prep, and no one knows anything about them."

"I know they didn't" said Polly quickly. "They had to go to Ma—Miss Burnett for returned history, so someone told me, so I didn't bother about them."

"Miss Burnett has been in Armiford all the afternoon and evening, and just got back. She knows *nothing* about them, and nor does anyone else," Monica informed her with more earnestness than good grammar. "Matey missed them at Junior supper and asked where they were, and Kathie Robertson—you know that mop-headed kid from Edinburgh?—told her they were with Miss Burnett, and Matey knew they'd been nothing of the sort for she'd just seen her. So she sent to look for them, and they can't be found—not anywhere, so we're going to make up search parties to go and look for them, and you'd better all buck up a bit!"

Having ended this long and somewhat confused speech, Monica vanished again, and they heard her racing back downstairs, even as they dropped their books and pens, and made ready to go in search of the missing trio. Only Cornelia, noticing Robin's sudden whiteness, slipped an arm round the younger girl to say with a reassuring squeeze, "Don't worry, Rob. They can't be far, and Gwensi knows the place like a book, I guess. You come and hunt with me, and when we find 'em, I'll tell 'em exactly what I think of 'em—the little—*coots*!"

"Better see that Bill or the Abbess isn't anywhere within hearing, then," warned Robin with a wavering smile as she went out of the room with Cornelia's arm still round her. "I know you, Corney! And after this bit of mischief, none of the staff will be feeling any too sweet." On which they rounded the corner, and ran straight into Miss Wilson!

CHAPTER 14

Intrepid Explorers

When the Third Form trio had left the bowling green safely behind them, Daisy, who was generally their leader, dragged the other two into a safe corner by the stump of an old elm on which she sat.

"What's up with Betty and Co?" she demanded.

"How do you mean?" asked Beth.

"Well, why did they suddenly want to ask Gwen about secret passages? They've never taken all that much interest in the place before."

"Some mad idea, I suppose. They didn't get much change out of her, anyhow. *You* saw to that."

"I don't like Betty Wynne-Davies," replied Daisy. "And I *know* she has something up her sleeve. I'd like to know what it is."

"Go and ask her," suggested Beth with a grin.

"Is it likely? Gwen! Haven't you any idea at all?"

Gwensi shook her head. "Not one. Anyhow, there *aren't* any secret passages here—not as far's I know, anyhow. The only place—well, I'll show you. But you must swear you'll never give it away."

"Of course we won't! Go on, Gwen! What is it?"

For reply, Gwensi caught hold of a hand of each of them, and pulled them away up the shrubbery to the kitchen garden. Arrived there, she led them past the great vegetable beds, now full of green things, and so to the very end to the great yew hedge. Here she paused, and looked carefully round. "I don't want anyone else to see us," she explained.

"There's not a soul in sight," replied Daisy after peering round the Jerusalem artichokes with the air of a conspirator of the deepest dye.

"You're *sure*?"

"Absolutely certain. Go on, Gwensi! The prep bell will

ring in about ten minutes' time, and we'll have to go.''

Thus commanded, Gwensi gave a final look round, and then stooped at a place where there was a small gap in the hedge. Into this she crawled, and the other two were not slow to follow. They made a snail-like progress along a narrow green tunnel, from where they finally emerged into a kind of cave in the yew trees, where there was just room for them all to kneel together.

"This is my secret place," said Gwensi a little shyly. She was a reserved child, and even to Daisy and Beth who had become such dear friends she found it difficult to divulge her long-hidden secret.

The pair looked round with approval. "It's a smashing place," said Daisy. "No one else knows of it but you? Oh, *good*! Then we can use it for secret meetings and all sorts of things. Does the passage end here, Gwen, or does it go on?''

"It goes on, but I've never bothered to explore much further. You see," went on Gwensi, settling herself as comfortably as she could in the restricted place, "whenever I wanted to get away from people, I always came here. No one ever found it out, and I was afraid there might be a place where I could be seen if I went on, and then they'd know about it. So I just didn't bother.''

"*I* see." Daisy nodded. "All the same, it might be rather interesting to know where it *did* come out, mightn't it? Beth, what's the time? I left my watch in my desk before we came out.''

Beth cast a casual glance at her watch. It was none too easy to see in the greenish light that came through the trees, but she was just able to make out where the hands pointed, so she said, "Ten past three. We've a quarter of an hour yet before we need to go in. Come on! Let's explore.''

Accordingly, they set off again, Daisy taking the lead this time.

"We can't go an awful lot further," she said as she crawled in. "The hedge doesn't go much further, does it?''

"The *yew* hedge doesn't. But it joins on to the old hornbeam thicket at the far end. I don't know if you can get through that. I've never tried." Gwensi spoke under difficulties, for an intrusive twig had got tangled in her hair, and she was having her own troubles over releasing it.

"Well, we'll try now. You all right, Bethy?"

"Quite. But do you think we'd better talk? People might hear us."

There was common sense in this remark, as both Daisy and Gwensi were quick to realize, so the remainder of the crawl through the yew hedge was conducted in more or less silence, an occasional "Ouch!" being the most that anyone had to say.

The end of the yew hedge opened, as Gwensi had suggested, into a large thicket of hornbeam which, as the trio learned later on, was of great age. Here they were stopped for the moment, for the tunnel, though still existent, was not wide enough to admit of their passing through, even Gwensi, the smallest of the three, shaking her head when she saw its narrowness.

Not that they were to be deterred by a mere detail of that kind! Daisy, the Guide, produced her Guide-knife, without which she never went far, and proceeded to hack away at the branches as well as she could, while the other two, by dint of stretching round and over her, broke off branches until at length they had cleared a way of sorts for themselves.

"All the same, I'll bet we'll tear ourselves," said Beth.

"Oh, well, we'll have to do some extra mending, that's all," said Daisy comfortably.

Beth said no more, but she thought it over. The eldest of a large family, where money was scarce, she knew that frocks were not too easily come by; and she was wearing her school uniform of brown-and-white check gingham, with its wide collar and cuffs of white cambric, and the school tie. The frock was practically new, and if it were torn, there would be trouble for her.

"I'm going to get out of mine." she said. "We'll find it easier to get through there, anyhow, if we haven't any skirts to bother about."

124

The other two saw the force of this. With a good deal of wriggling they contrived to get out of their frocks, which they folded up, and pushed well to the side of the hedge to be out of the way. In their anxiety, they pushed them so far, that a small part of Gwensi's skirt peeped through the thick stems, and later on caused much heart-searching to the people hunting for them with ever-increasing worry.

However, that was some hours ahead. Now, the intrepid explorers having wriggled free of their hampering skirts, found it a comparatively easy matter to struggle through the narrow opening and worm their way into the heart of the thicket, where, most unexpectedly, they found themselves in a kind of round chamber, plainly cut by hand, for no trees would ever have grown in just that particular shape of themselves. It had a cone-shaped roof, and was high enough for even long-legged Daisy to stand upright.

"Well!" exclaimed that damsel, as she looked round, "we *have* made a find! I wonder who keeps it like this, though? Can you get out anywhere, d'you think?"

They scouted round, and then Beth uttered a low cry of triumph as she pointed to a place where the ground shelved down, apparently to the roots. "There's an underground passage! I'm sure of it! Oh! Can't you see what's happening? It's through here that the Spy comes to make signals! That's how he gets up here—and gets away too, of course!"

With one accord, Daisy and Gwensi came to her side, flinging themselves on their knees to peer down into the uninviting tunnel which ran downwards into the earth. It was little more than a huge burrow, but quite big enough for a small man or a schoolgirl to crawl down. Naturally the trio prepared to crawl down it without the faintest idea of any danger to themselves. All thoughts of preparation had long since faded from their minds; and in the semi-twilight in which they had been the changing of the light was no reminder to them. Even their stomachs gave them no hint of the passing of time, for in their excitement they forgot to feel hungry.

"I wish we'd had the sense to bring a torch or two," said

Daisy, as she once more prepared to head the expedition. "I suppose you two haven't any matches and a candle-end or so about you?"

"We're in our Liberties and our knicks," Gwensi reminded her simply.

"But even if we'd had our frocks, I don't cart matches and candles about with me," added Beth.

Daisy grunted. But she saw that if they meant to follow this adventure to its end, they must go on in the darkness and trust to luck to getting through all right. She wasn't prepared to give up when they had got so far. So, with a last warning, "Well, follow me, and don't be in too much of a hurry or you may get kicked!" she proceeded on hands and knees down the tunnel.

For about ten minutes they went in a black darkness that might have frightened them wholesomely had they not been so intent on their quest. Then, to their amazement, they came out suddenly into a pit of some depth, the edges of which were protected by a mass of gorse. Here, they found unmistakable signs of human occupation. An old tin can, still quite serviceable, stood at one side of the pit; and in a deep recess near at hand were the ashes of a wood-fire: a couple of tins of salmon and one of peaches reminded them that they were hungry, and, all at once, they began to think of the time.

"Whatever time is it?" demanded Daisy.

Beth looked down at her watch. "Ten past three—but it *can't* be! It was that the last time I looked at it, and that's ages ago!" She raised her wrist to her ear and listened. "The wretched thing's stopped! Goodness knows what time it is! Frightfully late, I should say—*What's that*?"

Instinctively, they all stiffened, and listened hard. There was no mistake. Someone was coming—two someones, to judge by the sound of the footsteps and the gruff voices that came indistinctly to them. Like rabbits, they looked frantically round for bolt-holes. The sensible thing would have been to go back up the earth tunnel. But for no known reason, the sensible thing was the one thing they never thought of. Instead, Gwensi made a dive for an opening on the further side, and the other two were after her in a flash. They found themselves in another tunnel which curved round almost at once, and here, round the bend, they waited to see what would happen.

What did happen proved to be a bad disappointment for them. What they had expected goodness only knows. Beth, later on, said that she wouldn't have been surprised if a parachutist had suddenly dropped into the pit from a "Jerry". Daisy and Gwensi were less explicit. However, all that happened was that two smallish, dark men clad in ragged velveteen trousers and old cloth jackets whose sides bulged suspiciously came into the pit, apparently from yet another tunnel, for they certainly did not fall from the skies. They were talking a queer, guttural tongue which Daisy knew was not German, though the inexperienced Beth at once leapt to the conclusion that it was, and was suitably thrilled at the thought that they were now close to "the Spy". Gwensi, needless to state, at once recognized it for Welsh, and listened as hard as she could.

The first few sentences gave the whole show away to her and, in her disgust, she gave vent to a snort which clearly reached the precious pair in the pit, for they swung round, and made for the entrance where the girls were hidden.

It was quite enough. With wild yells, the trio turned and fled into the darkness, the men after them, and the next ten minutes were very uncomfortable for everyone. It ended in Beth's floundering into a pool of stone-cold water up to the waist, and her anguished shriek and the sound of the splash she made brought the other two to a standstill, so that the pursuers easily caught them up. Then, while one of the men grabbed the shoulders of Daisy and Gwensi, the other took Beth by the wrist and hauled her out, wet, shivering, and almost on the verge of tears.

This man spoke a brief word to his companion, and, prisoners of war, the trio were led back to the pit, where one of the men uttered an exclamation of horror when he saw Gwensi.

"Miss Gwensi fach!"

Gwensi lifted her head, her dark eyes blazing, and her cheeks scarlet. "Owen Owens! You unpatriotic *beast*! So it's you who's been showing lights and signals to those German brutes!"

"Indeed, Miss Gwensi fach, I have not. Look you, I would rather be cut into little pieces. But a rabbit, or a hare—where's the harm?"

"It's stealing," put in Daisy, who was considerably more frightened than Gwensi, for she had no idea who the men were—though her friend obviously knew one of them, since she had called him by his name. All the same, Daisy was the eldest, and she had not the smallest intention of resigning the leadership of the expedition. Besides, Joey had told her to look after Gwensi, and she was going to do it to the best of her ability.

The Welshman glanced at her, and his next speech, still made to Gwensi, was in his own language. The two English girls could make nothing of it, though they heard his "Miss Gwensi fach" repeated more than once, and gathered that he was pleading with Gwensi.

That young lady stood perfectly still, her small head erect. When Owen Owens had finished she answered him with a brief word of negation, and he turned to his companion, who spoke rapidly. Gwensi interrupted him vehemently, and what she said annoyed him, for he gave her a lowering scowl, and said something else, at which his companion shook his head. The argument became a quarrel between the two men, Owen Owens evidently refusing something his mate wanted. Finally, they ceased talking, and Gwensi turned to her chums.

"They are Owen Owens who lives up in the mountains at Tyfairweli," she said, "and his cousin, Griffith Owens. They've been poaching—rabbits and hares; and, sometimes, salmon. They have flares, and hold them low over the water, you know, and the salmon come to the light—it's all in *The Water-Babies*. This is their hide-out, and they want us to promise that we won't give them away. I s'pose it's them who've been showing lights—but I think the soldiers are great idiots not to have caught them before this. Only, they say that path we ran down leads to the river, and they hunt from there—all among the undergrowth; and they haven't been able to do it lately. I say I'm jolly well going to tell unless they'll promise me to give it up and go into the army. They don't want to. Griffith Owens doesn't, anyhow. I think Owen would, 'cos his wife was a friend of Megan's before she got married. Griffith says if we won't do as they say, they'll keep us here, tied up, until they can get away. It would mean prison for them, of course, if we gave them away. Griffith would hate that. His mother was a gypsy, and he can't bear to live in a house, much less Armiford gaol. If they'd promise to join up, I'd agree, but if *they* won't, *I* won't.''

"Neither will we!" Daisy was determined. "They're unpatriotic pigs and they've been showing lights for their horrid salmon-poaching, and they might have brought the Germans on us and we'd be bombed! I'm going to tell the Abbess and get her to send for that Colonel Black man as soon as ever we get home—so there!"

Griffith Owens listened to this tirade with an unpleasant smile. Then he said something to his cousin, at which Owen Owens uttered a grunt or two. Gwensi listened, and dismay came into her face.

"What is it, Gwen?" asked Daisy anxiously.

"Griffith Owens wants to take us up the mountains for two days to give them a chance to clear out," breathed Gwensi under cover of the new argument going on between the cousins. "They could do it all right. Ernest's always said, 'Trust a poacher to know how to get about without being seen!' They've ways of their own. If they do, what on earth will everyone think? The Abbess will be scared stiff—"

"*Mummy!*" broke in Beth. "Auntie J. said we must try to be extra good so that she wasn't worried because she isn't awfully fit yet. Gwen, you must stop them doing that! Do you hear? It might kill her! Promise you'll say nothing for two days, and then they'll let us go."

Owen Owens heard her and swung round. "Will you do that?" he asked, his black eyes snapping in the fading light which was going rapidly in the pit.

"If we do, will you take us home—or let us go back by the tunnels?" demanded Daisy.

"Yes, but you must all three swear that for two days you will say nothing whatever."

"We'll do it!—Daisy—Gwen! You can't say 'No!' Think what it may mean to Mummy!" pleaded Beth, tears standing in her eyes.

It went badly against the grain for the other two to give in; but Beth was so urgent that at last they did. They promised that for two days they would say nothing. After that, they would insist on telling Miss Annersley and, probably, Colonel Black. And, in return, the two men agreed to take them back to the garden and to show no more lights.

Thus it was that at ten o'clock, when everyone was growing steadily more and more frantic as time passed and the truants had not turned up, though their frocks had been discovered where they had left them, through the end of the yew hedge, and Megan was convinced that gypsies had run off with all three—though why the said gypsies should have taken off their frocks and left them, she was unable to say—the intrepid explorers arrived at Plas Howell, very dishevelled, very grimy, very hungry, and tired out; but quite safe.

Matron took charge of them, and whisked them off to hot baths, bread and butter and milk, and bed, while Miss Annersley, after phoning the news to the Chesters and Jo, sank back in her chair, mopped her face with her handkerchief, and observed pathetically to Miss Wilson who was with her, "I feel as if I had been put through the mangle several times in the course of the last few hours. *Is* my hair quite white yet, Nell? It feels as if it ought to be."

CHAPTER 15

The Death-Wail

The school was slumbering. In the San, Daisy, Beth, and Gwensi were fast asleep, tired out with all their adventures. In the dormitories, even Cornelia, Polly, and Robin, who had stayed awake some time discussing the evil deeds of their Juniors, had dropped off; while in the pretty room which had been reserved for her, Miss Annersley was dreaming peacefully. Down in the village, Jo Maynard, having attended to the wants of her daughters for the last time that night, was curled up on her pillows, her long black lashes making heavy shadows against her tanned cheeks. In short, it was night at its quietest. Only the sound of the wind through the leafy trees of late June, the trill of a nightingale in a far-off thicket, and the distant drone of an aeroplane, keeping watch and ward far above, broke the stillness which reigned over all.

Suddenly, just as Robin was dreaming that she was back on the loved Tiernsee in a small boat with Joey, Daisy, and Rufus, Jo's big St Bernard, while the triplets tried to catch fish with their toes, a hideous noise crashed out. Thin, eerie, and horrible, it swelled high, to die away, only to come back with renewed vigour, startling quiet sleepers awake, frightening the children, and making the men, who knew what it might mean, curse loud and long at a foe that could stoop to such despicable methods as the bombing of women and children in the hope of breaking down the country's morale.

At the school, the first to rouse was Miss Wilson. Always a light sleeper, she was out of bed before the second blast from the siren had got well on with it, and was feeling for her slippers and dressing gown. "So it's come at last, has it?" she muttered to herself as she got into them, and then hurriedly drew the thick blackout curtains she had drawn before going to sleep. "There! That's better! Now I can see what I'm doing."

She fled from the room, and went racing down the long corridor to the dormitory where cries told her that the girls were also awake now. She was joined by Miss Lecoutier, whose usually quiet eyes were blazing at this sudden wakening, and Miss Phipps, who was flying to rescue her beloved babies from the fear that might possess them. At full speed the trio made the round of the dormitories and bedrooms, bidding the girls get up at once, pulling the blackout curtains close before they switched on the lights, that the children might be able to grab their clothes always laid ready for such an emergency, and then leaving most of the rooms to the care of their own prefects. On the whole, the school reacted finely to it all. They had had air raid drill several times, and knew exactly what to do. Catching up their bundles of clothes in one hand, each girl seized on the small suitcase which stood by her bed, containing a complete change, washing materials, and any special treasures, and then joined the line at the door, from where the prefect marched them downstairs to the cellars, three of which had been prepared as shelters. The Head had heard so many pitiful tales of folk who had been bombed out with nothing but what they wore that she had insisted that the girls must have these light cases ready in case of need.

Meanwhile, she herself, leaving the girls to the staff, hurried down to the library, where she snatched the cases containing important papers belonging to the school, and followed down to the shelters. There she handed them over to Rosalie Dene, one of the first girls to join the Chalet School in its infancy, and now the school's secretary, and went back for other valuables. Miss Wilson and Miss Phipps stayed with the girls, after seeing that the emergency exits to the cellars were open in case of need. The rest of the resident staff followed the Head to secure those things which they all wanted to preserve if it were possible.

The girls, once they were safely down, were inclined to look on the whole thing as rather a good joke. Even the very

132

little ones, who had been startled and frightened by the hideous braying of the siren, caught the infection, and began to laugh as they dressed quickly. The prefects, who had scrambled into their own clothes in record time, gave a helping hand where it was needed; and the people most in need of soothing turned out to be one or two of the maids, who were sure the planes were on them, and they were all doomed to death at once, if not sooner, to quote Cornelia, who was here, there, and everywhere at one and the same moment.

Said Elizabeth Arnett to Betty Wynne-Davies as they combed out their untidy heads, "I say, Bets! D'you remember what Mrs Russell said that first day we were in Guernsey—term before last, I mean?"

"No, what was it?" demanded Betty.

"Why, that we'd need all our courage, and we must jolly well stick whatever lay before us. *Don't* you remember? What a sieve you've got for a memory. I can just hear her saying it now."

"Well—what about it?" asked Betty peevishly. "Why d'you suddenly think of it now—except that if Jerry comes chucking his bombs about we certainly *shall* need to stick it."

Elizabeth nodded. "That's what I was thinking—and also if she had any idea that this sort of thing was likely to happen."

"She was a schoolgirl in the last war, wasn't she? Didn't they have air raids then, too? I expect she went through them and remembered them."

"What's that?" asked Cornelia, who had passed the pair closely enough to catch part of this talk. "Of course they had air raids in the last war. But who d'you mean went through them?"

"Madame. She did, didn't she? I mean, she'd be about that age?"

"Oh, yes. She told us about them during that time we were in Guernsey after our crowd escaped from the Nazis from the Tyrol. Jo asked her one night, if she thought the raids would be as bad or worse than those she'd been through."

"What did she say?" asked Elizabeth, her arm round Betty.

Cornelia glanced round. At least a dozen of the girls had been attracted by the chatter, and were listening eagerly. "Said she was afraid they'd be worse, but she guessed she could trust Chalet School girls to behave like Britons," she replied. "After all, Elizabeth, if we can't, our training here couldn't amount to much, could it? But we all know we've got to show the grit in us. I guess this is the time to show it."

"Suppose they bomb the house and it collapses on us?" said Betty fearfully. "It *might* happen, you know."

"In that case, I guess we'd not only have moral grit to show in us, but physical, too," said Cornelia calmly. "Don't be a little fool, Betty. Even if such a thing did happen and one part of the house caught it, they wouldn't be likely to waste more than *one* bomb over us, and it might quite likely be one of the far wings. We're more or less under the great staircase here. And look how all the place has been shored up! *And* the emergency doors! They're all open this minute, and we could get out all right. So pull yourself together, do! It hasn't happened yet, and it probably won't. The siren only means that German planes are hanging about in the area, and I guess the British'll soon chase them off."

With this, she left them to go and see to Gwensi who was having difficulty with her trousers—the girls were all in gardening kit, the Head having ordained this to save any trouble with flying skirts—and the Middles were left to themselves for the time being.

"It's pretty hard lines on Joey down there in the village with those three babies," observed Myfanwy Davies at this point. "Has she a proper shelter, does anyone know? For she'll only have the maid, as Robin and Daisy are both here, thanks to those three making idiots of themselves today— or is it tomorrow yet? I wonder where they got to? No one has heard anything yet, have they?"

"I reckon Betty's idiot question sent them haring off after some hidden passage of their own," said Mary Shand wisely. "Oh, I know Gwensi said she didn't know of any, but likely she remembered something and they found one by accident. Anyhow, the Abbess will get it out of 'em tomorrow, you may be pretty sure. Wonder where they got to?"

"Girls! All of you go and sit down over there," said Miss Wilson's voice at this moment. "The prefects are bringing round milk and biscuits for you in a minute or two. Hurry up, Fourth Form!"

The Fourth turned and made for the lines of sleeping-bags which had been set out in the centre of the cellar, and sat down on them, one girl to each bag, and waited for the milk and biscuits hopefully.

"A midnight!" said Mary Shaw cheerfully. "It's a bit different from my first midnight. That was a mess-up, I'll tell the world!"

"It certainly was. You were jolly sick after it," said Betty unkindly. "And Joyce Linton nearly died—I've heard some of the others say so."

"I say! Gillian and Joyce are all alone in that little cottage of theirs," put in Biddy O'Ryan. "Oh, it's meself is sorry for them!"

"I'd forgotten them." Elizabeth's face clouded. She had begun to develop a warm affection for gentle Gillian Linton who was so adored by the Kindergarten. Gillian's pansy-blue eyes and long black plaits swung round her head in a coronal appealed to the rather wild Middle; and besides this, Elizabeth was absorbing the atmosphere of the school in these troubled days as she might not have done in normal times. Now she looked at Biddy, and spoke almost sharply. "Are you sure they're alone, Bids?"

"Oh, yes. They've only got a woman who comes in the morning. Joey sees to the rest of the work while Gillian is up here," said Biddy. "I know, because Joyce told me so when I went there to tea last Saturday. She said she was getting practice for the time when she had her own house to run, and she was learning quite a good deal."

135

Elizabeth said no more, but the cloud stayed on her face. Betty glanced at her curiously. Of the pair, who had been almost the worst firebrands the school had ever known—and one could scarcely have said it had been exactly free from them—Elizabeth was the more thoughtful. Betty had always been a handful, and even now, at almost fifteen, she was almost childishly tiresome. Elizabeth, two or three months older, was beginning to think for herself. Betty felt this and she did not like it. It meant that her chum was growing away from her. That her best plan would be to try to grow with her never occurred to her, and a feeling of resentment rose in the younger girl's heart as she saw the other's troubled eyes. They had always been together since they had first gone to St Scholastika's School at the Tiernsee—the school which, on the retirement of its Head, had joined up with the Chalet. They had been one in mischief, in form, in games. Was she to lose her friend? She slipped a hand through her arm and gave her a little shake.

"The Lintons will be all right. You needn't worry about your beloved Gillian like that," she said sharply. "What's got you, Liz? You never used to be like this. Snap out of it—do!"

Elizabeth looked down at her—she was half a head taller than Betty now—and she shook her head before freeing herself. "You don't understand, Bets. And it's rather awful for Gillian. It's only three years since Mrs Linton died—not three years yet. Gill's had to be mother to Joyce, and she's had lots of trouble for years. It's hard lines having this sort of thing on top of everything else."

Betty took her hand away with a scowl which lasted even when Robin brought her milk and biscuits. She forgot to say "Thank you" to the prefect, but Robin was preoccupied with wondering how Jo was getting on and never noticed. Besides, manners were not things you expected from Betty Wynne-Davies. She passed on, and the two Fourth Formers partook of their milk and biscuits in silence.

The silence was suddenly broken by a crash. Cries arose

from some of the younger girls, but most of the others set their teeth. It *might* not have been a bomb. That hope was quickly dispelled by the sound of another, and yet another.

"Jerry's being busy tonight," said Polly Heriot from her corner.

"Isn't he?" agreed Robin after a quick glance across the room where Daisy was sitting beside Beth and Gwensi. "Let's hope it's all so much wasted time. It doesn't *sound* very near, does it?"

"I don't think it is," said Miss Wilson, who had come into the cellar, and was sitting munching biscuits in company with Miss Lecoutier and Rosalie Dene. "I don't know, of course, how far sound—" A violent concussion interrupted her, and the house seemed to rock. Some of the maids screamed again, and one or two of the little ones burst into tears, but the others sat tight—metaphorically, at any rate. Actually, Robin jumped up from her lowly seat and ran across the cellar to Daisy, putting one arm round her and one round Gwensi.

"Sorry I haven't a third for you, Bethy," she said with a shaky laugh. "Come and sit in my lap, though, and then you won't feel so out of it. Come along, chérie."

Beth huddled up at her feet, and laid her chestnut head down on the proffered lap. "I hope it won't upset Mummy. Jo told me—she isn't—very strong yet," she said unevenly.

Daisy flung an arm across her friend's shoulders. "Don't worry, Beth. God will look after your Mummy. We'll ask Him, shall we, us four?"

"Yes, it's the best thing we can do," agreed Robin. "Let's say our prayers hard for a minute or two. Then I expect the Abbess will be down and want us to have sing-song or something."

So the four girls closed their eyes, and prayed silently but fervently for those they loved, as well as for Mrs Chester. All round the room other people were doing the same, for that last crash had been unpleasantly near, and many of them were wondering just how near the next would be. Then the door opened, and Miss Annersley came in, accompanied by Mr Denny, the school's singing-master, and his sister, who was responsible for various oddments, such as Italian, junior geography and history, and grammar.

"They're bombing over Newport and Cardiff way," she said.

"That last effort wasn't there, surely?" asked Cornelia. "It sounded mighty close—*mighty* close! I'd have said half a mile or so away at the very most if I'd have been asked. They must be using heavy stuff if it's as far away as Cardiff. How far are we from there, anyone?"

No one answered her, for Mr Denny had strolled forward. "We may be forced to stay here some time—nay, even, it may be, many hours," he began—and Betty Wynne-Davies, despite the seriousness of the position, choked as usual over his Elizabethan diction—"Let us, therefore, show our courage and our pride by beguiling the time with a song. Come, little maids, one and all. Gather round, and we will sing the song that speaks so bravely of our England."

The girls gathered from this that he wanted them to sing Parry's "England". They congregated together round him, squatting cross-legged on the floor, and the staff joined them. The maids huddled together close at hand, and drawing a tuning-fork from his pocket, he gave them the key-note, singing a melodious "La-ah!" before he raised his hand to conduct them. Then, like one voice, it came forth:

"This royal throne of kings; this sceptred island;
This earth of majesty; this seat of Mars;
This fortress built by Nature for her service
Against infection and the hand of wars."

The girls sang well, for they had been well trained, and the song was a favourite at any time. Sung under such conditions, it held far more meaning for them than it had ever done. Even graceless Betty Wynne-Davies forgot her giggles as she joined in.

138

It was punctuated by crashes, more distant than the one that had rocked the house and startled them all, but quite alarming enough. The German army was out to break the British morale if it could, and went at the work with all its evil might. Now and then a mistress would steal out of the cellars by one of the emergency doors to make sure that all was well outside, for Miss Annersley had been able to murmur to those nearest that the bombers were using incendiaries as well as high explosive, and they all knew that incendiaries were unlikely to draw attention to themselves by any violent thuds. They could see the lights flashing in the dark skies, and a dull red glow far away in the southwest told them that fires must have broken out. But so far Plas Howell was unharmed.

On one of these expeditions, while the girls, having finished "England" and sung through "You'll Get There" and Bunyan's Pilgrim Song, were clamouring for "On Wings of Song", Miss Annersley stood on the great lawn before the house looking upward at the roof and clustering chimneys. Miss Wilson was at the back doing the same. Fire-watchers had not yet been established, for this was the early months of the "Blitzkrieg"; but the Chalet School authorities had no mind to be caught napping. As the Head stood there, anxiety on her pale face, something came hurtling down from the heavens, falling within six yards of her. With an exclamation she sprang back, fully expecting an explosion, and forgetting all rules for such an emergency in the shock. But nothing happened, so she pulled herself together, and approached the object lying in the shallow hole it had made for itself in its fall. She saw a small cylinder with a long streamer attached, and in the light of the full moon she could make out white letters on the black material of the streamer. Bending forward, she saw in printed lettering the words "Schule Chaleten". The Chalet School! What on earth did this mean?

There is no excuse for Miss Annersley. She certainly ought not to have done any such thing. But such was her excitement, she forgot all military orders and all precautions and picked the thing up. Then, after a final glance up at the roof, for another German plane was choking its way across, she pulled at the streamer, and at once a rolled paper came out of the cylinder. Wondering what on earth she held, the Head entered the house as speedily as she could and ran to the library, where the closed shutters and thick velvet curtains made it impossible for any light to get out. There she switched on the light after she had shut the door, and then eagerly unrolled the paper. It held two or three lines of printed script. Very simply it said, "Chalet School, hail! The brother of two old girls greets you. They have bid him tell you they will never forget the Chalet School Peace League, and they will love you always. Their brother joins them, though he is forced into this abomination. Karl Linders."

Emmie and Joanna Linders! Miss Annersley caught her breath as she recalled the two German girls who had been such favourites in the school where they had been for some years. Bonny girls they had been, with their flaxen locks, blue eyes, and startlingly black eyebrows and eyelashes. How were they faring, she wondered, in Nazi Germany. She knew that their father had been taken before a tribunal more than once and threatened with the concentration camp for his political views. She had hoped that he and his family had managed to escape before the war; but it was evident that they had not, since Karl was flying in the Luftwaffe. Poor Karl! She had known him in the old days, a handsome, jolly lad of fifteen or sixteen. He must be nineteen now. He had always told her how he hated Hitler and all his works, and now he was forced to do Hitler's evil work. Tears came to the Head's eyes as she realized how this boy must be feeling. Then she remembered that her duty lay with the girls under her present care, and rubbed them away before she went to rejoin them. She showed Bill the communication, and Bill gasped when she saw it. But neither of them could discuss it there. Some of the tinies were getting very sleepy, and one or two had actually dozed off. The singing had ended, for even the elder girls were getting tired.

"Best get them into the sleeping bags and let them sleep if

140

they can," suggested Matron in an undertone. "I don't know how long this is going on; but it's nearly two, and they'll be like a lot of wet rags tomorrow if they sit up much longer."

Miss Annersley agreed with this remark. She clapped her hands for attention, and when they were all looking at her, she said with what gaiety she could assume, "Girls! The Germans seem to be going to make a night of it. I think we should all feel better if we took a nap. Get into your sleeping bags, and let us see how comfy they are. Prefects, help the little ones to pack in. Fourth and Fifth, you can manage for yourselves, can't you? We'll wake you if it seems necessary."

Rousing a little, the girls began to get into their sleeping-bags.

"Shades of our expedition to Salzburg!" said Cornelia to Elizabeth as she passed that young lady on her way to tuck a small First Former safely in. "Do you remember how we all sprawled along the seats of that coach when we were on the way home in the thunderstorm?"

"Yes," said Elizabeth sombrely. "It was good fun, then. And we had Jo, and Louise, and Gillian with us, too."

"You and your Gillian!" interrupted Betty rudely. "You think Gillian Linton's the cat's eyelashes, don't you, Liz? You *are* a fool."

Elizabeth flushed to the roots of her red hair, but she said nothing. Cornelia glanced at her. Then she took the matter firmly in hand. "Shows her sense and her good taste, I guess. Gill Linton is one of the greatest girls I know. 'Tisn't everyone who could face up to what she's had to face up to and come through it as she has! First of all, the trouble about Mrs Linton's illness; then her death; then having to leave their home in the Tyrol and start all over again. And Joyce was all she had, and Joyce is engaged and will be getting married before long. Gill will be alone then. But she's making no fuss about it. She's taking it just as she's taken everything else. I guess if ever I respected a girl, I respect her."

Then she went on to see to little Claire Duhammel. But later on, when she and the other prefects were discussing the night's events together, she observed, "I shouldn't be surprised if we hadn't seen the end of our troubles with Elizabeth Arnett, anyhow. That little ass Betty Wynne-Davies will be a nuisance—she's born to be hanged, that kid. But Elizabeth's improving at the rate of no man's business, I guess."

Meanwhile, silence fell on the cellar, as one after another, soothed by the warmth and comfort of the sleeping bags, drowsed off. When the "All clear!" came about three o'clock, only the Head, Miss Wilson, and Matron were awake to look at each other with sighs of relief. The raid was over and their precious charges were safe.

"All the same," said Matron as she bestirred herself to make a cup of tea for themselves, "I'd like to know what that one particular crash was. I gave us all up for lost for a moment, I don't mind telling you."

"I felt pretty much the same myself," yawned Bill. "Isn't that kettle of yours boiling *yet*, Matey? What ages it takes! Hilda, what do we do about the girls? Wake them and get them back to bed? Or leave them to have their sleep out?"

"Oh, leave them, I should say," said Matron. "More than half the night is over. It'll be well on to five before they're all in bed again if we wake them and drag them upstairs now. They're warm and comfortable and safe where they are, and sleeping in their clothes for *one* night isn't going to harm them. Hand me that teapot, Nell. My kettle's ready in spite of your maligning it as you did. We'll have our tea, and then I vote we try and get a snooze ourselves. I'm pretty well all in."

"I could do with a nap," confessed Bill, rubbing her eyes. "Thank you, Matey! What a blessing tea is! However should we get on without it? Speaking for myself, I'd rather have a cup of tea to face an emergency with than any another drink you liked to name."

"What English from a member of staff!" teased Miss

Annersley, who could smile now that it was all over. "Very well, Matey, we'll take your advice. I'll just run up and make sure all the doors are locked, and then we'll retire ourselves, I think."

An hour later, not a soul in the house was awake, for even Matey, the ever-vigilant, was snoring happily in a corner of the far cellar, a beatific smile on her face, and her nose buried in her blanket.

CHAPTER 16

Next Day

Retribution of various sorts fell next day. To begin with, everyone felt stiff and uncomfortable on waking up. Even with sleeping bags, the floor is not the best of mattresses, and most people groaned over their stiffness. Then sleeping in clothes, even if you are wearing trousers, is a messy business. Most of the little ones were cross as a result of their broken night, and the Middles were also affected. Indeed, Betty Wynne-Davies and Elizabeth celebrated the affair by a violent quarrel, Betty having chosen to jeer at her friend's anxiety over Gillian Linton's welfare. Naturally, Elizabeth retorted, and before three minutes were over they were in the thick of it. That they were caught using most unparliamentary language by Gillian herself and duly scolded did not mend matters in the least. In the end they parted, Betty vowing that Elizabeth was "a soppy ass", and Elizabeth replying with rather more dignity that Betty was a mere child who could not be expected to understand.

Daisy, Beth, and Gwensi were called to account for their doings of the previous day by the Head, who rebuked them soundly for going off as they had done and giving everyone so many hours of worry. They also had to tell their tale to Colonel Black, who came over posthaste on getting the Head's telephone message, and gave them to understand that they were silly little girls and great nuisances. What their duty had been was to tell someone with common sense what they had discovered, when he and his men would have investigated, and the precious pair of poachers might have been laid by the heels. As it was, they were probably miles away by this time and going scot free. He hoped— h'rrumph!—that their teacher—at which Miss Annersley looked annoyed—would punish them well for their bad behaviour. Meanwhile he could tell them that they had probably been helping the enemy, for it was all very well to tell three foolish children a whole pack of lies; but who knew what the men had really been up to? Spies they almost certainly were—h'rrumph!

At this soothing statement, Gwensi's hot temper flared up. "Indeed and to goodness then, but they would not tell *me* lies!" she flared out, rather more Welsh than usual. "And you are a liar yourself to say so!"

More fireworks, once the Colonel had recovered from the shock of being spoken to like this by a small girl! He was not surprised that the war had broken out! When silly babies could speak like this to their elders and betters— h'rrumph!—no less was to be expected!

He was interrupted by Miss Annersley, who said sternly, "Gwensi! You forget yourself! Apologize to Colonel Black at once for your rudeness! I am ashamed of you!"

"I *won't* apologize!" cried Gwensi, stamping her foot. "I won't—I *won't*! He's no right to say such things! He's only an Englishman—what does he know about us? Owen Owens would never lie to me!"

Of course, Miss Annersley recognized that Gwensi's temper was mainly the result of over-tiredness; but she could scarcely overlook such defiance, so she said, "Gwensi, go straight to Matron and say you are to go to bed. You must have taken leave of your senses. As for you, Beth and Daisy, you may go, too. I am sure Gwensi would never so far forget herself unless you two had been encouraging her. Go at once. I will make your apologies to the Colonel myself; for if *you* aren't ashamed of giving so much trouble, *I* am ashamed for you."

Gwensi burst into tears, an example Beth and Daisy were not far from following, and the three departed bedwards, convinced that the Colonel was the nastiest old man who was ever made—I quote Daisy—and the Head was just as mean for punishing them at all. That it was scarcely meant for a punishment, but was an excuse for helping them to make up their lost sleep without laying too much emphasis on it, never dawned on the trio.

When they had gone, the Head made what apologies she could to the Colonel for the shocking behaviour of her pupils. He accepted them with sundry comments about "Spoilt modern children—don't know what the world is coming to—never been spoken to like that in my life—h'rrumph!" But he accepted them. Then the Head turned to another question which had been troubling her very much.

"Colonel Black, there was one bad crash—it sounded very close at hand. Can you tell me anything about it? And can you tell me if we are fairly safe here; or do you advise me to have air raid shelters dug for the girls? Naturally, I feel very anxious about them. They are always a big responsibility; but in war it is doubled. What do you advise?"

Clever Miss Annersley! There was nothing the Colonel liked so much as being asked for advice, and he promptly gave it. Certainly they were as safe where they were at Plas Howell as anywhere in England. The bomb which had alarmed them all so much had fallen in a field about half a mile away. Two rabbits had been killed—at least, bits of two rabbits had been found. There might have been others—no one could say. As for the shelters—might he see the cellars before he gave his advice?

Certainly he might. Miss Annersley rose from her chair and led him off to them at once, thankful to have steered away from the wicked trio.

"We are using three of the cellars under the centre of the house," she explained as she took him downstairs. "As you see, the ceilings have been well shored up; and there are three emergency exits, as well as the passage with the stairs down which we have come, and another flight at the other end. What do you think, Colonel? Will the girls be reasonably safe here? Or do you think I had better have shelters dug? I am not anxious to have to take the girls outside. Last night was warm and dry; but if it were wet, or if we had bad raids in the winter, it would be a very different thing. Still, I must do the best I can for them."

The Colonel went round the three cellars carefully,

146

examined the emergency exits with their doors opening out-wards, and finally gave it as his opinion that the cellars were as good air raid shelters as could be desired. Still, if she felt nervous, the best plan would be to have two or three dug at some distance from the house. He suggested that they should go out and choose a spot, and then she could tell the men to begin that day. The sooner the better if it was to be done.

So the school was regaled with the sight of the Head, accompanied by the Colonel, now cooing like a wood-dove, making her way round the grounds to seek a good site for extra shelters to be dug. Not that the school bothered its head about the reason for the promenade. The girls gave their own reasons for this—some of them libellous.

"He's so mad with those three," declared Cornelia, "that she's got to take him to the kitchen garden and offer him all our best fruit and veg to soothe him down."

"If that's the case, I hope he gets tummy ache—greedy old wretch!" said Polly Heriot with feeling.

"More likely to be for his men," said Jeanne de Marné. "I should not think he would eat much fruit. He looks a beefy, muttony man to me." At which description the Sixth forgot its troubles and shrieked with laughter.

In the Fifth, the general opinion was that the Head was going to have anti-aircraft gun emplacements built round the house to keep the Jerries away—a sensational sug-gestion made by Enid Sothern and adopted eagerly by all her clan. Incidentally, when presently the men began to dig for the air raid shelters, the Fifth said, "I told you so!" to all and sundry. They were not allowed to forget this a little later on when the real reason for the digging came to light.

In the Fourth, Betty Wynne-Davies, who could be out-rageously vulgar when she chose, came out with the idea that the Colonel was in love with the Head and this was his way of courting her.

"Rats!" said Biddy O'Ryan. "He's a married man with six children this minute. How would he be wanting another wife, I ask ye?"

"Who told you so?" demanded Betty, rather crestfallen at this.

"Joey herself when I was telling her about him," returned Biddy calmly. "So you're wrong for once, Betty Wynne-Davies."

"For *once*?" echoed Elizabeth. "She's wrong most of the time. And if any of the staff heard you talking like that, you'd get into nice trouble the lot of you. I never heard such disgusting talk in my life!"

Such remarks coming from Elizabeth, of all people, so startled the Fourth, that they forgot the cause of their argument and turned to look at her with amazement in their faces.

"Is it ill you are?" demanded Biddy, the first to recover from the shock. "Maybe it's the sun too hot on her head, and she wearing no hat."

"She must be sick—or mad," agreed Mary Shand with conviction. "I reckon the night in the cellars has upset her. Maybe we should tell Matey."

Elizabeth flushed. "I'm neither sick nor mad," she returned crisply. "But I do loathe such talk—it's cheap. Joey would hate it, and so would Madame. And you all know it!"

"Joey and Madame? Sure you don't mean dear Gillian?" put in Betty viciously.

"No, I don't! I mean Joey and Madame. All the staff, too. *Any*one would who even pretended to be a lady."

"Oh! So I can't even 'pretend' to be a lady!" Betty's quickly-roused temper was up in arms at once. "I wonder you ever condescended to be my friend, Elizabeth Arnett, since you think I'm not a lady!"

Once again, Elizabeth scored. "I never said that. And I'm certainly not going to quarrel with you on such a point. Biddy, have you seen the Third's asparagus bed lately? It's doing splendidly. Come with me and see it now."

Dumb with surprise, Biddy allowed herself to be walked off, and the Fourth were left gaping at this sudden change of face on the part of Elizabeth. Even Betty found nothing to say at the moment; though she declared later that Elizabeth Arnett was going "all goody-good and pi", and must have been reading the Elsie books.

The small people had too much to think about to trouble their heads about the doings of their elders, and the two people chiefly concerned never knew how much interest their innocent stroll had roused. They inspected various sites, all within reasonable distance of the school, and the Colonel finally fixed on a part of the garden that sloped steeply upwards toward the summit of the hill which rose some way at the back of the house. As he pointed out, even if they got a direct hit it would be impossible for a bomb to reach them. The shelters must be carefully dug and propped with the greatest care. But if this were done, he thought the place would be completely safe. "And as it is on a slope, any water caused by heavy rains or snow will drain away from the shelter, so it cannot become water-logged," he pointed out. "If you really wish to have earth shelters, I think you can scarcely be safer than here. I should advise digging four at intervals round the slope of the hill. I believe you are a large number?"

"Over eighty girls, and then the staff and the domestic staff," replied the Head. "Do you think it would be possible to arrange to have sleeping places like berths or bunks in them? We all slept on the floor last night, and it is not too comfortable. I am afraid most of us are not really rested, and tempers are frayed as a result—which," she added, "accounts, I think, for Gwensi Howell's extraordinary outburst just now. I do apologize, Colonel. It is not in the least like her."

The Colonel had recovered his own temper by this time. "I quite understand," he said. "Just a bit of childish impatience. Think no more of it, please. And now, about this question of bunks. I think it a very good idea—very good indeed. I see no reason why it should not be possible. I suppose you would have them two deep round the walls?"

Miss Annersley agreed, and after a little more talk the Colonel took his departure, and she returned to the house, where she was met with the information that Joey and her babies were awaiting her in the library. The Head nodded, and hurried down the hall to the big, pleasant room in which Joey sat, her precious triplets in a chair beside her, buried in a book.

"My dear Jo!" cried the Head, "I am so sorry I was out when you came, but I was busy with Colonel Black. Gwensi had ruffled his feathers pretty badly, and I had to do something to smooth him down."

"So I heard," replied Jo with a grin. "I've seen Robin, and she, apparently, met the three going up to bed, and got the whole tale from Daisy. I hope, Hilda, you'll let me take my pair home now. It was on the lonely side without them last night—not to speak of worrying."

"You knew that we should look after them, Jo?"

"Oh, yes. But I'd rather have had them under my own eye. You know what Rob means to me. And Daisy is almost as dear, now I've had her to myself all this time. I'd only Anna to help me out with the babes. I've come to fetch Daisy and Rob—and also to bring you some news," she added as the Head sat down, taking baby Len in her arms.

"News, Joey? Pleasant, I hope?"

"*Very* pleasant, I think. First of all, Jack gets leave next week."

"That *is* good news. He'll see a difference in his daughters, won't he?" And the Head laughed as she looked down at the bonny baby she was cuddling. "They were tiny when he went away."

Jo nodded. "He hasn't seen them since he went away after Christmas. They were barely two months old then. They'll be eight months by the time he arrives. They were born on the third of November, you remember? Yes, they've grown rather. And they've each got a tooth or so to show Papa when he lands. They're rather nice altogether, aren't they?"

The Head laughed again. "Joey, you're as proud of your triplets as a peacock with two tails. You know what lovely babies they are. I don't think even David and Sybil were as pretty—or Josette. Which reminds me: do you know how Madame got through the night with all that crowd on her hands? The small fry haven't turned up today; but when I tried to ring her, I couldn't get through. Are they all right?''

"Perfectly. I called there on my way here. Jem was there. He and the rest arrived in England three days ago, but they had to do all sorts of official things about the San as soon as they landed, so he sent no word home, as he hadn't an idea when they'd be able to get away. I gather that he merely walked in at tea-time yesterday, and startled Madge out of ten years' growth. He looks fit and well but rather tired. I think they had a bit of a job to get away at the last. And then they couldn't come straight here—they had to go to Ireland first. Madge is one rapturous beam. You know she'd heard nothing since the very beginning of May, and the anxiety has been telling on her. I've got Bruno coming later on today. He had to stay in town to finish up some loose ends of business. And I've got a fine surprise for him. Frieda came back this morning. He was only to break the journey here, you know, and then go on to the Isle of Man to join her. However, it's all right. I haven't warned him," she added with another of her schoolgirl grins. "I thought he could stand a little shock of that kind all right."

"I expect he could," agreed Miss Annersley. "Well, is that the end of your news?"

"Don't you think it's enough?"

"It's fairly lengthy, I admit. But—I know you, Jo. What have you still got up your sleeve?"

"Only that they're thinking of establishing the San among the Welsh mountains. So if they do that, we'll have it near us again—or fairly near, anyhow. The infants will have to weekly-board, I expect. It'll be about fifteen miles as the crow flies from here, but a good deal longer by road. Then David is to go to a boys' school next term—but Madge will tell you about all that herself. Rix is going as well. You'll keep Jackie for another year, though. But it's time David and Rix were among boys. Why, Rix is nine, and David is seven, now. Jem says it's the Cathedral School for them for the next few years. After that, they must go to public school—supposing any of us have any money for such a luxury by that time. At the rate things are going up, I should say we'll all be reduced to taking in each other's washing to make a living as they say the Scilly Islanders do,'' she added with an infectious laugh.

The Head joined in. ''I hope it won't be so bad as all that,'' she said seriously then. ''After all, Joey, we have a lot for which to be thankful. I know we had a nasty experience last night, but those poor folk in Cardiff and Newport had a much worse one. I do feel we are about as safe here as we can be. And that reminds me, I haven't told you *my* piece of news yet. See here!'' And she produced the cylinder and its contents which she had found the previous night.

Jo inspected them closely. ''Karl Linders! Emmie's and Joanna's brother!'' she ejaculated. ''How on earth did he know where to drop it?''

''We've been discussing that. My own idea is that he didn't—didn't know, I mean. I expect they've got wind of our removal to this part of the world somehow, and he dropped it about here on the chance that it would get to us sooner or later.'' And, as they discovered two months later when young Linders crashed into the sea and was taken prisoner—and a very joyful prisoner, too, despite his broken leg—that was exactly what had happened. Joey and Jack went to see him, and he told her how Emmie and Joanna were doing their best to keep the Chalet School flag flying in Nazi Germany, as well as many another Old Girl of the Chalet School, and he was able to give them news of quite a number. His parents were dead, and the two girls lived with an uncle and aunt who would be kind to them. He hoped that it might be possible for them to get out of Germany some time, but he could not see when. However, all this happened in September, and at the moment, it was just the end of June, and Joey was sitting reading Karl's letter with eager eyes.

''Well!'' she said when she had finished it. ''Does the school know?''

"Nell and the rest of the staff, of course," said the Head. "I haven't told the girls yet. There's really been no time. But I will do so at Prayers tonight. I'll tell you of the excitement on the phone later," she added, laughing. "What—are you going already?"

Joey nodded as she picked up a baby in each arm. "Yes—must! Anna is insisting on a thorough clean down as Jack is coming home, and I left her up to the neck in it. If we want any lunch at all today, I shall have to see to it myself. Send for Daisy and Rob, Hilda, there's a dear! I don't think I could go through another night like last night again in a hurry. Mercifully, the babes slept through most of it. I wish they'd hurry up and do something about gas masks for babies. I'm in dread of those brutes using gas. Anne Chester says the same, now she has little Janice. And Madge has Josette to worry about and Janie has Barney. Oh, what a world it is! And all because of one man's ambition!"

"That is probably very much what your great-great-great-grandmother said at the time of the Napoleonic Wars," returned Miss Annersley drily.

"Napoleon didn't use poison gas, and he didn't bomb helpless cities either," retorted Jo, firing up in defence of that other would-be world conqueror who had always been a hero of hers.

"Aeroplanes and poison gas weren't invented in his time. We can't know what he would have done with them if they had been," replied the Head, ringing the bell. "Shall I carry Len out for you? How did you come? Oh, Gladys, would you ask Matron to get Miss Daisy up and send her to Mrs Maynard in the garden? And ask Miss Robin to get ready to go home, too, please. You'd rather be outside, wouldn't you, Joey?"

"Yes, thank you. As for how we came, I have a little petrol, so I brought the car. But I've got to be careful, you know. I'm trying to save towards the winter, for I don't want to have to let the girls weekly-board; and if we have bad weather, that's what it'll mean. I could scarcely let them cycle through heavy snow all that distance."

"But you won't be alone if Jack is here. He'll be with you most of the time," said Miss Annersley soothingly, as they passed through the great hall and out into the sunny garden, where Jo's little runabout stood before the wide, circular steps.

"My dear Hilda! Jack's a doctor! He'll spend a good deal of his time over at the San. He won't let me go there because he wants the babies to have the first years of their lives unclouded by the sight of suffering, so he says we're better where we are, and he'll be with me as much as possible—that's if the army lets him go. I don't know; they may not. I shouldn't think they would. I don't expect it."

"Well, anyhow, you'll be in the same country. That's better than having him in France."

"You never know. They may send him out East." Jo was in a thoroughly pessimistic mood, largely the result of her bad night. However, the sight of Robin tearing across the lawn to her with outstretched arms made her stop thinking about it and hurriedly deposit her twin burdens in safety in the car before she turned to clasp her darling closely to her.

"Rob! Are you ready, my precious? I've been telling Hilda all the news which you and Daisy have to hear as yet, while you've been doing whatever it was you were doing. We're only waiting for that bad child now. Then we're all going home and, this afternoon, we're taking to our beds. We all need it, I'm sure. Let me look at you properly, my Robin. I only saw you in the hall when I came, and it's shadowy there." Jo turned the slight, dark-eyed girl who was so near to her heart so that the glorious sunshine fell on the lovely face beneath its curly mop, and scanned it with loving, anxious eyes. "Yes, just a wee bit tired, aren't you, my darling? A nap won't come amiss for any of us. And here comes Daisy!"—as that long-legged live-wire came darting through the hall to fling herself with a wild whoop on Jo, regardless of the Head who was standing near, smiling, Len still in her arms.

"Joey darling! I *thought* you'd come! Oh, Joey! Wasn't

154

it a ghastly night?—but funny, too," she added, as she released Jo to go to the car and pick up little Connie. "How did the babies like it?"

"Oh, they howled a bit when that *fearful* crash came—the one that nobbled a rabbit or two, I hear," said Jo casually. "Beyond that, they slept through most of it. But I'm having you two home at nights from now on—definitely. And Joyce and Gillian are coming to sleep at our house. They can have the big guest room. Oh, by the way, Frieda has come back, and Bruno is coming tomorrow. I've put them into your room, Rob, so you must share with Daisy for the present. Frieda is furnishing those three big attics at the top, so that she'll have a little flat for Bruno to come to when he gets leave, so it's only for this once. And Jack's coming home next week—the end of the week—for seven days' leave. So we'll be full, all things considered."

"We will. How lovely to have Frieda again! Give me Len, please, Miss Annersley. I'll hold her till we get home." And Robin, already seated in the car, held out her arms and took Baby Len from the Head. Daisy scrambled in beside her, and demanded *her* special pet, little Margot, who had been named for Daisy's own mother. Jo cast a laughing glance at Connie, the middle one of the three. "Poor scrap! Does no one want my pet Connie? Never mind, precious. Wait till we get home and Mamma will love you all right. You settled behind there? Right! Shut the door—er—*Miss Annersley*, please!" She flashed a wicked glance at the Head, who knew very well that Jo had only just stopped using her baptismal name before the girls, and burst into laughter, even as she complied with the request. Then Jo started up, and a minute later, was bowling down the wide drive in clouds of white dust, chuckling to herself, and the two schoolgirls, carefully holding their respective babies, were eagerly plying her with questions about all the latest news, and Daisy, at any rate, was pouring out information of the wild adventure she and Beth and Gwensi had undertaken the previous day, and the wonderful discovery they had made, as well as Colonel Black's visit and its sequel—so far as they were concerned.

At the school the Head went back to her work, and was soon as busy as she could be. Nevertheless, she found time amongst all her activities to wonder first, why Betty Wynne-Davies was going about wrapped in gloom and why Elizabeth Arnett had suddenly developed such a fondness for her work that she could not even see her erstwhile chum during the Shakespeare lesson.

CHAPTER 17

Growing Pains

To the unbounded amazement of the school, the coolness between Elizabeth and Betty continued. Elizabeth was developing quickly in these days, and, as Cornelia once remarked, you could almost see her changing before your very eyes. Her rather hard little face became softer, more gentle. Her manner lost its aggressiveness and abruptness, and her voice began to deepen in tone. Along with these physical changes came mental ones. She took a greater interest in her work; and, from being a thorn in the side of anyone who taught her, was becoming an interesting pupil. She thought things out more and began to reason for herself. Previously she had looked on lessons as something to be got through somehow. If a mistress was able to entertain her, so much the better; she was quite willing to be entertained. But work had been another question. Now she showed signs of being on the science side, and her botany papers, from being the bane of Bill's existence, became objects of real pleasure.

The school at large realized all this some days before the staff did. Then, one evening when they were marking work on the terrace, Miss Wilson looked up from her folding desk to remark, "How that child Elizabeth Arnett has improved lately! This exercise of hers on oxygen in nature is really quite good—excellent, for her. And her diagrams are also good."

Simone Lecoutier glanced up from the Sixth Form French compositions. "You think so? Well, I have been astounded by her translations lately. They are doing *La Dernière Classe* this term, and Elizabeth has made something really good out of the first page of "L'enfant Espion". I was amazed, I can assure you; for you know how badly she has always done."

"I shall look forward to having her again," said little Mademoiselle de Lachenais, who had spent most of the term in a nursing home recovering from a bad appendicitis operation, and had just returned to the school. Simone had been taking some of her classes in French while she was absent, and a Miss Smith from Armiford had come out daily to see to the Junior mathematics. Jeanne de Lachenais was not yet allowed to do any work, for she had had a bad time and was still far from strong. But, during the past week, she had insisted on mingling with her colleagues, and was trying to persuade the Head to let her set her own exam papers.

Simone nodded. "You will be interested, Jeanne. You know how we have all despaired of her. Never, even when Corney and her crew were Middles, have we had a more tiresome girl than Elizabeth. And by the time Corney was fifteen, she was Senior Middle prefect, and quite a responsible person at St Clare's—"

"Do you remember the band she and her crowd got together?" asked Jo, who was with them, sitting in a low basket chair, while her daughters sprawled on a big rug at her feet. "*And* the concert they gave us at the end of term? I nearly died of hysterics on the spot."

Bill, laying down her red-ink pen, nodded. "I've never ached so much in my life! You and your crew were enough to turn anyone's hair grey, Jo; but Corney and Evvy and Co went one worse. Still, they were nice children at heart, and that's what I thought Elizabeth and Betty and all that throng never would be. I can't say I see much difference in Betty either," she added. "By the way, she seems very much out of sorts just now. Anyone know what's gone wrong with her?"

Simone nodded her head sagely. "It is that Elizabeth is growing up and Betty is not," she said. "Betty feels she is losing her friend, and she is miserable about it."

Jo glanced across at her. "You think so? I've rather wondered from what Rob tells me at times."

"What does Robin say?" demanded Simone. "I have

only just noticed the change in Elizabeth myself, though I have seen that Betty was not happy lately, and wondered why. But it is so difficult to ask them.''

"It was the other night," said Jo, stooping to pick up little Margot and remove a leaf from her mouth. "Bad girl! you mustn't eat leaves. Aren't they *awful* at this age? Every blessed thing goes to their mouths. The night after the raid, I think it was, Rob had finished her work and was sitting beside me for a little before we went to bed. Suddenly, she said, 'Elizabeth Arnett is changing. She's growing up. I wonder what Betty will do about it.' I said, 'Grow up, too, I expect. She can't remain a baby all her life. It's time she did something about it.' Rob shook her head and said that Betty wasn't altering at all, and she didn't think she even wanted to.''

"Really?" Miss Wilson looked interested. "Has anyone else noticed at all?"

"Beyond the fact that Betty is going round looking as if she had lost every friend she had in the world and is a perfect nuisance in class, I can't say I've noticed her much," said Mary Burnett, speaking for the first time. "I sent her to the Head for rudeness this morning. She really was the limit. We were doing the wind-up of Warren Hastings in India, and halfway through, she leaned across to Biddy O'Ryan—who, I am thankful to say, took no notice of her—and said, quite loudly, too, 'I think this is the most boring lesson I've ever known, don't you?' And then she looked at me and yawned! I could have boxed her ears! However, I sent her to the Abbess with a note, and I should think she got it hot and strong, for I hear she was remarkably subdued when she came to Miss Smith's lesson.''

"Was she gone all that time?" asked Joey.

"She was. I told the Abbess I refused to have her in any more of my lessons for the rest of the term.''

Jo whistled as she put her baby back on the rug. "A bit drastic, wasn't it? What did the Abbess say about it?''

"Said she fully agreed with me, and until Betty apologizes for her rudeness she will not come to my classes but work by herself at the punishment desk in the hall. It's not a pleasant outlook for Betty.''

"Punishment desk?" Jo looked puzzled. "What on earth is this?"

"Oh, haven't we told you? It's the latest. If anyone behaves in a anti-social way, she is removed from society, and sent to the punishment desk in the hall. That means that she has to work alone. She has also to be alone for free times, and eat alone. It generally works quite well, but I can't say it's had much effect on Betty so far. She really is the limit! And she's close on fifteen, too. It's more than time that she came to her senses!" Mary sounded quite fierce as she spoke, and Jo laughed.

"Then what about Elizabeth? What has worked the reformation with her? Has she had the punishment desk *ad lib*, or what?"

Mary shook her head. "Nobody knows, my dear. It's been going on, so far as I can tell, for the last two or three weeks—perhaps a month. But it *is* a reformation; there's no doubt about that. She's not the same child. She really is beginning to work; and she's lost that unpleasant sneering manner she had. Myself, I date it from the night of the air raid. It was after that that I noticed anything."

Simone glanced across the terrace to where Gillian Linton was sitting with her lap full of raffia mats belonging to the babies. "I can tell you one thing at least. Gillian has something to do with it."

Gillian looked up and stared at her. "*I* have something to do with Elizabeth's reformation? What rubbish are you talking, Simone? I've never had anything much to do with the child—except in the way of pulling her up for her many sins. I admit I've done my fair share there."

"Well, I've heard Betty jeering at her about you," replied Simone. "She called you, 'Your darling Gillian', and was really very nasty. I couldn't interfere. For one thing, it would not do. For another, I was not supposed to hear. But Betty has a most unpleasant tongue."

Gillian blushed to the roots of her black hair. "What

utter rot! Do you expect me to believe that Elizabeth Arnett, of all people, is turning soppy? I don't believe it! What did she say to Betty?"

"Nothing—but nothing at all," returned Simone impressively. "She waited till Betty had finished, and then walked away—I heard her."

"But where were you to hear all this?" asked Jo with interest.

"In the bathroom—the one with the broken fan-light. I did not like to come out on them; so I stayed where I was. But you know how shrilly Betty speaks when she is angry. I couldn't help hearing." Simone spoke defensively, and Jo laughed. "Don't get upset, my lamb. No one ever suspected you of deliberate eavesdropping."

"I hope not. I despise such a thing—to listen at doors to what is not intended for one! Such a thing is despicable. But I could not cover my ears, for I had been dyeing my blue frock, and my hands were all blue. They still are." And Simone extended a pair of daintily-kept hands that were bright azure blue in parts, though parts were clean.

"I'll give you something to clean them," said Bill sympathetically. "Yes, I agree. You could scarcely clap hands like that over your ears. You *would* have been a pretty sight if you had! Well! I must say this is news to me."She looked at Gillian thoughtfully. "It strikes me, Gillian, my child, that you have a big responsibility towards that girl. If she really is beginning an affection for you, you can do a lot for her."

"And you ought to do it," added Jo. "Elizabeth Arnett is a girl of strong character. If you can make her a decent member of the community you'll deserve a vote of thanks from everyone else. I remember what she was like that first term that St Scholastika's joined up with the Chalet School." She stopped, and chuckled. "Does anyone here know about that play of theirs on the roof of St Clare's?"

"Play on the roof of St Clare's?" Miss Wilson sat bolt upright. "What are you talking about, Jo? *Who* had a play on the roof?"

"Oh Gemini! I forgot you knew nothing about it. I

suppose, in the rush of events after that, no one ever thought of telling you. Well, it's all years ago, so it won't matter your knowing now. It was the term Lulu Redfield was Head Girl, you may remember. The prees had found that some of the Middles were in the habit of getting out on the roof at night—it was flat, as you may remember—and disporting themselves. So they got permission to sit up to catch them—though I know you never knew exactly *why*.''

"I remember. Go on, please. This is interesting and all new to me." Bill looked alertly across at Jo, who gave another chuckle.

"Well, I dropped in on them—I forget why I was hanging about the school at that time of night; I think I must have been spending the evening somewhere and got belated. Anyhow, they were all in your study, so I joined the happy throng, and when they'd got going, we stalked up the stairs and caught the lot. Never shall I forget their faces when we all landed among them! They were giving a play written by Elizabeth, and Lulu made them give it to the school at large. Talk about laughing over Corney's band! You nearly had to carry me out from that play!" And Jo rocked in her seat as she remembered that very funny tragedy.

Bill nodded. "Of course! I remember it all now. We all nearly passed out. Do you remember the duel between the hero and the villain when the elastic in the top of the knickers of one of them suddenly gave and she had to finish her fight holding on to them?''

At this pathetic picture, the whole staff shrieked with mirth, and Jo nearly rolled off her chair among her babies. When she had recovered herself, she sat up, wiping her eyes, and remarked, "Well, Elizabeth was the moving spirit there. You know, that kid had brains all right. If she's beginning to apply them in the proper direction, and you, Gill, can give her a helping hand, I think you ought. But you say that Betty is no better? You know, I'm sorry for that kid. She sees her bosom pal growing away from her, and she doesn't want to walk in the same direction and she's being hurt pretty badly. What can you do about it?''

"Nothing," said Miss Wilson gravely. "Betty isn't a girl who can be reasoned with. Anything in the way of a change there must come from herself. At present, as you say, Jo, she's resenting the change in Elizabeth, and she doesn't understand that if she wants to keep her friend she must walk with her. No one can do anything, for she wouldn't listen to us; and I doubt if the rest of the clan can see through things. They are all more or less in the puppy stage. Elizabeth is the oldest of them. Biddy O'Ryan is definitely a child. She is younger than her fourteen years. It's a nice youngness—not like Betty's, of course. But she could give no help of that kind to anyone. As for the rest—Jack le Pelley, Isabel Allan, Terry Prosser, and all that crowd— they are younger than Elizabeth and Betty, and most unlikely to help. Isabel, indeed, is two years younger than anyone else in the form; but we couldn't put her into Third. She's well up to the rest of the Fourth."

"Then what can you do about it?" asked Jo thoughtfully.

"Exactly nothing. Only wait and seize any opportunity that may occur—I don't quite know when that will be. At present, Betty is hating us all rather badly. But what can we do? She can't be allowed to behave as she has been doing. Apart from anything else, it's so bad for the rest."

Mary looked up. "You don't blame me for complaining, then?"

"Not in the least. No mistress would put up with such rudeness."

"Can't the prefects do anything?" asked Joey.

"You must talk to Robin about that. I think they can probably do far more than we can. They are her own generation, and very near her own age. You can't expect girls of Betty's age to want to confide in anyone as much older than herself as we are. I hope some of the prefects will take hold, as you say, and do something about it. The only thing I'm afraid of is that Corney, good as she is as Head Girl, has scarcely sufficient insight into character to tackle such a difficult problem. And Polly, Sigrid, Jeanne, Violet,

Lorenz—they are dear girls, but they are no wiser. Our best hope is Robin. She has always been older than her age; and then she lives with you, Joey, and I know you talk to her. See if you can slip in a word or two, won't you? She may be able to help Betty; but I don't think anyone else can—except Betty herself."

"I'll do what I can. It's a sticky problem as you say. Growing pains always are. And that, when you get to the bottom of it, is what's really wrong with them. Betty has 'em worse than most, I should say."

Jo got up and began to collect her babies. Simone came to help her, and the rest of the staff, after fond farewells, turned to their respective tasks. Only when the two chums were alone by the pram, packing in the small people, Joey lifted her eyes, dark and velvety as pansies, to her friend's face. "D'you agree, Simone? Do you think Rob can really help that child?"

Simone nodded. "I think she is the most probable person."

Jo looked troubled. "In one way I'm sorry. I don't want Rob burdened with too many troubles."

"No, my Jo. But she will always be meeting such problems, and she will always find something that can help. She is that kind—as *you* were. I have not forgotten how you helped me when I was a silly, jealous child. Rob will be like you."

Jo went beetroot red. "What utter rot!" She dropped into English, for they had been speaking French at the moment. "You were only a little un-understanding. You soon got over that, and we've always been chums, Simone—always will be. You, and Frieda, and Marie and I have always had a wonderful friendship. Even our marriages and your engagement have never spoilt it, as, so I'm told, such things do often spoil friendship."

"No!" Simone spoke quickly and vehemently. "For you have never made me feel alone and out of it. And now I have André, and before next term, please God, I, too, shall be a wife."

Luckily the babies were all safely in their pram. Jo caught her friend in her arms at these words. "Simone! Do you really mean it? When did you know? When is it to be? You'll be married from me, of course! Your own people are in Scotland, but they must come to us for it. We'll put them up among us. But I *must* have the bride!"

Half laughing, half crying, Simone replied, "I heard only this morning. And for my parents and Renée, there will scarcely be time for them to come here, for André wired this morning that he is coming the day after tomorrow, and we are to be wedded in the Catholic Church at Armiford the next day. I have sent them a telegram, but I have no hope that they will be able to reach us, for they are in the Highlands with Papa's cousin, and often they do not even get their wires till the next day. And oh, Joey! What am I to do for a dress?"

"I've got a length of white silk I've never used. And my own veil is floating around somewhere. We'll set to work at once. You come down first thing tomorrow, and we'll get going with it. Anna is a good needlewoman and she'll be thrilled to help. So will Frieda. Oh, Simone! What gorgeous news!" And Joey hugged her friend again. Then the babies began to yell, so she set off down the drive with them, reminding Simone to be at her house as early as possible next morning.

CHAPTER 18

Simone is Married

No one ever knew how the news got about, but get about it did. By the end of the day all the school knew that Simone—Miss Lecoutier—was expecting to be married on the Monday.

"And we haven't *time* to collect and buy her a decent present!" wailed Violet Allison in the privacy of the prefects' room.

"We can make the collection all right," said Cornelia. "It's getting anything in time. Why on earth didn't she give us even a *hint*? I wouldn't have believed it of Simone! Even Joey let us know when she got engaged. Frieda's wedding *was* different; but, then, look what happened just before. But Simone's been here all this time, and she's never said a word to anyone. I do think she's mean!"

"I think she only heard this morning," put in Jeanne de Marné shyly. "If that is so, Corney, she could not tell us. And we have all seen her engagement ring. We knew it must come some time soon."

"H'm! Well, perhaps you're right," conceded Cornelia. "All right; we'll say no more about that. But we *must* collect up at once. And it's end of term, of course, and no one will have a penny to spare; and there's no time to write home. Next week's exam-week? Has anyone realized that?"

"With all that's happening there hasn't been much time, has there?" asked Polly Heriot reasonably. "Well, I'm in funds, as it happens. Here's my contribution, Corney. My guardian sent me a pound note this morning. I guess, as you would say, I can manage on half that for once." And she produced a ten-shilling note which Cornelia joyfully grabbed.

"I can manage as much, so that gives us a good start off.

One thing Poppa never keeps me short of is money, thank goodness!''

"I can give you half a crown," said Violet, laying it on the notes.

"And so can I," added Sigrid; while Jeanne, daughter of an impoverished noble family, heaved a sigh, and produced a shilling. "I should gladly give more if I had it; but I have not."

"Guess it means as much and more than ours," declared Cornelia. "Thank you, Jeanne; it's jolly decent of you." And she cast an appreciative look at Jeanne, who felt that her sacrifice of chocolate for Simone was well worth it.

One by one they gave their quota, some more, some less. When she had got the entire Sixth's, Cornelia dealt out a form to each of the prefects and bade them gather up what they could. "Better limit it to sixpence a head," she said. "It's safest. We, of course, are different."

"We've most of us known Simone for years," agreed Sigrid. "She was a Senior Middle when I was a very small Junior in dear old Tyrol. Vicky has only known her this term, of course"—and she smiled at quiet Vicky McNab— "but she's doing extra maths with you, Vicky, so you've had a chance to get to know her which some of the others haven't."

"Yes, indeed!" said Vicky. "If I do well in maths at School Certificate it'll be owing to Miss Lecoutier. She's a great coach!"

Then they separated, those who had collecting to do to see what they could gather; the others to draw together and discuss what kind of papers they would be likely to get in the coming Oxford Examination. Seven of the Fifth and Sixth were taking School Certificate, and there were eight Junior Certificate. The events of the past few days had put such things as exams out of their heads; but now realization of the fact that the trial was almost on them came with a shock, and they talked eagerly. Previously, the school had taken no public exams. In the Tyrol, there had been no facilities for such things; and no one had been ready for the

Christmas examination. This was their first attempt as a school, and they were firmly resolved to do their best for the sake of the school as well as for themselves.

Meanwhile, knowing nothing about what was happening amongst the girls, Simone, in the staff room, was receiving wishes for future happiness and much teasing about her hurried wedding. She was afire with blushes, and finally fled to her own room, where she barricaded herself in, feeling thankful that Joey would be a refuge tomorrow. They would be too busy for any torment if a whole frock had to be made, even if Frieda and Anna were to help. No aid in sewing could be looked for from Joey. That young lady had always hated the very sight of a needle, and though the school had made her a very fair needlewoman, she always refused to touch one unnecessarily, though she prided herself on her knitting.

Next morning saw the whole school in a ferment. Simone escaped as soon as she could, and fled to Joey's pretty house near Howell Village, where she found that young lady all ready prepared, with big scissors, sundry paper patterns which might be adapted, a pile of odd pieces of lace, and the precious white silk. On a table in the corner lay her own bridal veil of old Venetian lace, the gift of two of her Italian friends, Luigia and Bianca di Ferrara. Frieda, happily married to young Dr von Ahlen, and now returned from her exile in the Isle of Man, met the bride-to-be at the door with warm kisses, and softly-uttered wishes for a similar happiness, and Simone felt with a sigh of relief that she had no teasing to fear here.

"It's a pity the triplets are too young to be your bridesmaids," said Jo as they sat down to a morning cup of coffee before getting to work. "However, I rang up Marie last night, and Maria Ileana and Keferl and her own little Wolferl will carry your trails. I knew you'd want some of our children, anyhow. And what about Rob for chief bridesmaid and Daisy and Peg and Bride with her? We could include Primula Mary if you liked. She's Bride's age, and they'd make a lovely contrast, one so fair and the other so dark. What do you say?"

Simone was quite willing to agree. "I had thought it must be a summer frock and hat and no bridesmaids, as all the rest of you have had," she said wistfully. "Even Frieda had Gisela's little girls. But Renée will never be able to get here in time, so I thought I must do without."

"Well, you won't," said Jo sturdily. "I rang Madge last night, too, and luckily her three—I include Primula Mary as hers, of course, though she *is* only a niece— so are Peg and Bride, if you come to that; but I do *not* advise you to have Sybil; your wedding wouldn't lack incident if you did, but I doubt if it would be a very peaceful affair!—her three have all new white frocks, and I've sent Rob and Daisy into Armiford with Marie to get what they could. Daisy is wildly excited, and we'll get on faster if she isn't here. Any more coffee, anyone? No? Then I'll just ring for Anna to clear and go out for a peep at the babies while you look over these patterns and see if we can make anything of any of them."

"Where are the babies? I want to see them," said Simone eagerly.

"Out in the garden in their pram. They're out all day now, of course. Come along, then—Oh, Anna, would you clear, please? Then you can get on with a free heart." This last to pleasant-faced Anna who had come into the room. Then, as Anna vanished with her tray, she added to the bride-elect, "Anna has begged off from sewing. She's making the wedding-cake."

"How *did* you get the materials?" cried Simone as she and Jo and Frieda went out to the sunny garden where the three babies lay in their big pram, sleeping the sound sleep of the healthy baby.

"I've been saving it when I could get it, in case any big occasion came along—like this, for instance. And we've heaps of raspberry-canes in the garden, and Anna has some wonderful idea of using the berries. I know nothing about it, so it's no use asking me."

When they went in after a due amount of babyworship, Frieda and Simone fell to work, while Joey, sitting down beside them, produced a handful of book-proofs and began

169

to correct. It took some time to decide; but finally they fixed on a picture-dress, with plain, many-gored skirt, and bodice, with a round neck which was to be adorned with a big berthe of Brussels lace which Jo produced from her stores. The veil would be fastened with a wreath of orange-blossom and myrtle, the former coming from the big hothouse which belonged to the house where the Russells had made their home, and the latter from a bush in Jo's own garden. "And I have new white stockings and my silver evening-slippers," said Simone joyously; "also a new set of undies, so I shall be all right. Jo, I am so grateful to you for all this. I know that it does not matter, and André will love me whatever I wear; but I am so glad that I shall *look* a bride as well as *be* one!"

Jo gave her a quick look. "You'd look it all right, my dear, even if you were married in your present rig. You couldn't help it with that look in your eyes."

Simone blushed furiously and dropped her long, black lashes over the said eyes. "What nonsense you can talk, Joey! But I *am* happy," she added rapturously. "And the best of it all is that I can stay with the school, for André will not be able to begin a new home at present. So I must try to get rooms nearby where he can come when he has leave, and come to school every day, as Gillian is doing. You will help me, won't you, Joey? For you know the people and I do not."

"Of course I will! I can give you an address this minute," returned Jo vigorously. "Mrs Evans at Hollands Court told me that she wished she could get a nice married couple for her vacant rooms, as otherwise she would have to take evacuees, and she's had such an experience with her last two sets she doesn't want another dose. *You and André shall be the nice couple.* It's only two miles away, and there's a bus runs past the gates of Plas Gwyn, so you'd only have the avenue to walk up. I know that may be a trial in bad wea-ther; but it would be possible."

"Do you really think she can have us?" asked Simone anxiously. "Oh, do you think—has she a telephone? Could you ring up at once in case someone else comes and takes them?"

Joey shook her head. "They haven't a phone in. But I'll send Anna up with a note, and bag them for you at once. Will that do?"

"Oh, very well! Thank you, Joey chérie, more than I can say!"

Joey laughed and went to her desk, where she proceeded to write an urgent note to Mrs Evans. Then she went to the kitchen to beg Anna to finish what she was doing and then go off on her bicycle to Hollands Court and wait for an answer. Anna agreed, and then Jo returned to her pretty sitting-room where Frieda and Simone were busily pinning the pattern to the silk.

"Anna will take it in an hour's time," she said. "Now, let's get on. I want to tell you my plans for Monday. You *have* wired to your people, haven't you, Simone? If they come, Madge will take them in and put them up for a few days. It would be fun to see them again, so I hope they'll be able to manage it somehow. Then we'll go into Armiford by car on Monday—you *have* fixed up for the licence and the priest?"

Simone nodded. "André saw about it all when he was last here. He will have wired to the Archbishop, and I rang up Father Vinton, and he said it was all right. We are to be married at eleven."

"Good! Then we'll come straight back here after the wedding and have as decent a wedding breakfast as Anna and Madge's Rosa can contrive. Are you and André having a honeymoon, may I ask? I won't say '*where*?' "

"Yes, but I could not say where if you *did* ask, Joey, for I do not know. André has arranged that, and Miss Annersley has given me all the week of his leave. It is good of her; for though it is exam week there is always plenty to do, and I have reports to write up. I am so grateful."

"Well, that's that, then. You can have my car, if you like. André drives, doesn't he?"

"Yes, but we are going by train somewhere. It is very

good of you, Joey dear, but no, thank you. Besides, what would you do?"

"Oh, I could manage for a week, my child. If it was anything very urgent, I could always bag Madge's little Hillman."

"No, Joey. It is very sweet of you, but I cannot agree."

Joey laughed and said no more. The work went on, and by the time Anna announced lunch the dress was well on the way. By eight o'clock at night it was mainly finished, thanks to yeoman's service from Madge, who came down in the afternoon from the big house on the hill, bringing Josette with her, and sewed industriously till six, when she had to go home for the baby's bedtime.

"Only the berthe to sew on, now; and we can do that any time," said Frieda joyously. "It *is* pretty, Simone. Will you come down tomorrow and try it on with the veil so that we may see how it looks?"

Simone agreed, and after a quiet little supper she mounted her bicycle and returned to the school. Sunday was a peaceful day, and when Monday morning came everyone was ready for the events of the day.

At school it began with a riotous breakfast from which the bride-to-be was absent, as the Head had sent hers up to her room with a gentle command to stay where she was until the car came to take her to Joey's where she was to dress. A wire came at nine, saying that the rest of the Lecoutier family would be unable to come in time for the wedding, but would be at Plas Howell to welcome the newly-married couple on their return from the honeymoon. Then Megan appeared, all beaming with smiles, to say that the car had come, and Simone, dressed in her blue cotton frock and big panama hat, picked up her suitcase and slipped off down the backstairs. She knew well enough that if she went by the front the entire school would be waiting for her, and she had no mind for that. Megan led her through the kitchen regions and round to the side of the house, where Joey's car, chauffeured by a lad from the village, was ready. She got in and was driven away. The school was just in time to see the tail of the car disappearing down the drive, and sent a united yell of disappointment after her. But they had little time for more, for the big coaches were coming for them at a quarter past ten, and Miss Wilson was among them, sternly ordering them upstairs to dress. They were all to go to the church, and then would meet in Joey's big garden, where that young lady had insisted they must be fêted as well as the rest of the guests. Meantime, Simone was being robed in the big front bedroom, where Joey, already in her fineries of soft blue georgette with big hat to match, and Frieda, sweet and fair in her delicate greens, helped her to arrange the veil, fastened a string of pearls round her throat, and put into her hands the big shower bouquet which Madge's gardener had been up at five to prepare. At last she was ready, and they clustered round her to give her their loving wishes and kisses.

"You look sweet, Simone!" said Joey earnestly. "Best wishes, darling! May you be as happy as I am! I can wish you nothing better."

"And as Bruno and I are," added Frieda, a very glad look in her eyes. "I wish you every happiness that we all have, Simone. I can say no more."

Simone looked at her. "I understand, Frieda. I am so glad—and so very happy, I shall cry if I try to say anything. Thank you both for all you have done for me."

"There's the car. We must all go!" cried Jo; "Jem never will wait a moment. Where are my precious babies? Look after them, Anna; and—" She got no further, for Jem himself was at the door demanding that they should hurry; so Joey kissed her babies, and then fled after the others to where Madge sat in her Hillman, while the doctor's big Napier stood waiting for him and the bride, for he was to give her away.

Of the drive to Armiford, Simone could tell no one anything later, though the doctor declared that they nearly had a bad skid, thanks to some cottage children rushing suddenly out into the road right in front of his bonnet. Lost in a happy dream, Simone saw nothing of it, and was only conscious they had reached the end of the journey when the car stopped and someone opened the door and helped her out. Then she was ascending the steps of the church on Jem's arm, and her bridesmaids were falling in behind her, and she was being led up the aisle to where André stood waiting for her, the short, slim airman who was acting as his best man behind him. He greeted her with a smile as she came to him through the crowded church, and then the service began, and Simone Marie Anne Lecoutier and André Jean Étienne de Bersac plighted their troth.

Simone's one sorrow was that her own people were not there; but she knew that they would be thinking of her, and when she and her new husband left the church her face was wreathed in smiles.

After that, the day went with a rush, till the honeymoon couple departed in Jem's car for Armiford, where they were to take the train to some place of which only the bride-groom knew, though he promised the younger portion of the company that they should hear later.

Finally, five o'clock saw Joey very tired but very happy, sitting down in a deckchair with Frieda, while Robin and Daisy played with the babies near by. All had changed into their everyday clothes, and all were relaxing. Anna had promised to bring a belated tea, and while they waited for it Frieda and Joey talked idly. Presently Frieda smiled.

"So the last of our old quartet is married," she said softly. "I am so glad. Simone is too dear and sweet to spend all her life teaching."

"So am I glad," replied Joey. "And the good old school is still going on, even though we are exiled and have had to remove again."

"I know," said her friend. "But the Chalet School is not only a *thing*, Joey. It is an *idea*—and a great idea. That can never fade."

"True. And so, whatever happens to us, the Chalet School must go on," agreed Jo.

The Chalet School
Series
ELINOR M. BRENT-DYER

Elinor M. Brent-Dyer has written many books about life at the famous alpine school. Follow the thrilling adventures of Joey, Mary-Lou and all the other well-loved characters in these delightful stories, available only in Armada.

Chalet School Three-in-One (containing The Chalet School in Exile, The Chalet School at War, and The Highland Twins at the Chalet School) £4.99

Armada

All these books are available at your local bookshop or newsagent, or can be ordered from the publisher. To order direct from the publishers just tick the title you want and fill in the form below:

Name _____

Address _____

_____

Send to: Collins Childrens Cash Sales
PO Box 11
Falmouth
Cornwall
TR10 9EN

Please enclose a cheque or postal order or debit my Visa/Access –

Credit card no:

Expiry date:

Signature:

– to the value of the cover price plus:

UK and BFPO: £1 for the first book and 20p per copy for each additional book ordered.

Overseas and Eire: £2.95 service charge.

ARMADA